Don't Tell a Soul

"Saved by the Bell" titles include:

Mark-Paul Gosselaar: Ultimate Gold
Mario Lopez: High-Voltage Star
Behind the Scenes at "Saved by the Bell"
Beauty and Fitness with "Saved by the Bell"
Dustin Diamond: Teen Star
The "Saved by the Bell" Date Book

Hot new fiction titles:

Bayside Madness
Zack Strikes Back
California Scheming
Girls' Night Out
Zack's Last Scam
Class Trip Chaos
That Old Zack Magic
Impeach Screech!
One Wild Weekend
Kelly's Hero
Don't Tell a Soul
Computer Confusion
Silver Spurs

Don't Tell a Soul

by Beth Cruise

Collier Books
Macmillan Publishing Company
New York
Maxwell Macmillan Canada
Toronto
Maxwell Macmillan International
New York Oxford Singapore Sydney

Collier Books
Macmillan Publishing Company
866 Third Avenue
New York, NY 10022

Maxwell Macmillan Canada, Inc.
1200 Eglinton Avenue East
Suite 200
Don Mills, Ontario M3C 3N1

Macmillan Publishing Company is part of the Maxwell Communication Group of Companies.
First Collier Books edition 1994
Printed in the United States of America
10 9 8 7 6 5 4 3 2 1

Library of Congress Cataloging-in-Publication Data
Cruise, Beth.
Don't tell a soul / by Beth Cruise. — 1st Collier Books ed.
p. cm.
Summary: The Bayside High gang is not sure if honesty is the best policy when Kelly tries to break into an acting career, despite a lack of natural talent, while Lisa discovers that one of the town's founders was a racist.
ISBN 0-02-042783-2
[1. Honesty—Fiction. 2. Acting—Fiction. 3. Prejudices—Fiction.]
I. Title.
Pz7.C88827Do 1994
[Fic]—dc 20 93-38917

To
all of Lisa's fans
around the world

Chapter 1

▼ ▲ ▼ ▲ ▼

On Friday afternoon, Lisa Turtle closed her locker door with a satisfying *clang.* Then she patted it for good measure. She wouldn't have to open it again until Monday morning at 7:33. Right now, that seemed very far away.

"What are you smiling about, Lisa?" Jessie Spano asked. She swung her long, curly ponytail behind her shoulder as she twirled the combination lock. "You look like the cat that swallowed the canary."

Lisa shuddered. "Ewww. Gross." She waved her hands vigorously in front of her face.

"What did I say?" Jessie asked, amused. "And what are you doing?"

"I'm waving away a negative thought," Lisa

said. "I got this image of a poor, defenseless little bird being gobbled up by a big, fat tiger cat. I'm waving it away. Negative thoughts make wrinkles. I read about it in *Find Your Inner Beauty in Twelve Easy Steps or Turn into a Very Old Hag.*"

Jessie giggled. "You're only seventeen, Lisa. Isn't it a little early to worry about wrinkles?"

"The book said that it's never too early to worry about your skin," Lisa said solemnly. "Now I'll replace the image with a positive thought. Mmmmmm. I'm slapping down my mother's credit card and buying that salmon pink outfit I saw at the mall. . . . " Lisa's mouth curved in a smile, and she gave a happy sigh.

Lisa considered shopping a serious matter. A trip to the mall involved rules, regulations, and rituals. It required discipline and sacrifice and timing. The only activity that could possibly compete with shopping was dating. One of these days, Lisa knew she'd be able to merge the two and find a boy who loved to shop. That would be heaven on earth.

Jessie's hazel eyes sparkled with amusement as she grabbed her books and shut her locker door. "You can't go through life waving away *every* negative thought, Lisa. There are too many things to worry about. There're bad grades and car trouble and pimples and the flu and being dateless on a Saturday night—"

"Stop, stop!" Lisa puffed. Her hands were windmilling furiously. "I can't keep up!"

Suddenly, Samuel "Screech" Powers appeared around the corner. He ran to Lisa's side in his size-eleven purple sneakers and began waving his arms in front of her face, too. But he tried to help so energetically that he wound up bopping her on the head.

"Ow!" Lisa said. "What are you *doing*, Screech?"

"I don't have a clue," Screech admitted, his frizzy curls bobbing as he continued to wave his hands in front of Lisa's face. "But I'd do anything for you. I'd climb the highest mountain, I'd swim the deepest sea—"

"Why don't you start right now?" Lisa asked sweetly.

He batted his stubby eyelashes at her. "I'd worship the ground you walk on, only these are my best pants."

Lisa gave a dubious glance at Screech's orange-striped overalls. "That's what scares me," she sighed.

Lisa was glad when their other best friends, Zack Morris and Kelly Kapowski, came around the corner carrying posters and a big roll of tape. Maybe they would divert Screech from his devotion. If that didn't work, maybe a major earthquake would come along.

"What have you got there, Kelly?" Lisa asked.

Kelly held up a cardboard poster from the stack she was carrying. "It's the announcement for this year's Bayside High Talent Contest. Ms. McCracken asked me to put them up."

"And I volunteered to help," Zack said.

"Whoa, hold the phone," Jessie said. "Did I hear Zack Morris say he *volunteered* for something?"

Everyone laughed. Zack schemed and scammed to get *out* of doing things. For him, attending school was just a temporary inconvenience.

Zack looked hurt. "What are you talking about, Jess? I volunteered to help a teacher last week."

Just then, A. C. Slater came up behind him. "That's right, preppy. You volunteered to help Coach Turk measure the cheerleaders for their new uniforms."

"Hey, I offered to give up my free period," Zack said, his hazel eyes innocent. He sighed. "So many waists, so little time."

"You're an example to all of us, Zack," Kelly said wryly. "Now hand me the masking tape."

"You're going to tape his mouth shut?" Slater said with a smirk. "It's about time."

Zack handed Kelly the tape, and she fastened the poster to the wall. "It should be a good contest this year," she said. "Greg Tolan wrote a new song he's going to play on his guitar. And Riley McGee is doing a sketch with Melissa Alden."

"I just hope Tony Berlando doesn't play the sax this year," Lisa said, shuddering.

"I wrote a song, too," Screech said. "And I'm going to enter."

"What are you talking about, Screech?" Lisa said. "Since when do you have any musical talent?"

"Oh, I don't," Screech said confidently. "But my computer is a virtuosi."

"Virtuoso," Jessie corrected.

"Gesundheit," Screech said.

"Ms. McCracken says that everyone has some kind of creative talent," Kelly said. She gave a rueful grin. "I sure hope she's right. I'll find out tonight."

"That's right," Jessie said. "Tonight is the first meeting of your acting seminar, right?"

Kelly nodded. "I'll be in class all day Saturday, too. And there're evening classes next week."

"Whoa, Morris," Slater said. "Sounds like it will be cutting in on your time."

"That's okay," Zack said. "I want Kelly to follow her dreams." He gave his girlfriend an affectionate look. "Besides, my dad's software company is starting up, and I promised to help. I'll be super busy, too."

"Kelly, how can you take a class on Friday night?" Lisa said. "Friday night is the time for the girls to hang together."

Kelly giggled. "Hang together? You've got to be kidding, Lisa. Don't you mean go out with you and watch you leave me sitting alone while you go flirt with guys?"

"You already have a boyfriend," Lisa said. "Don't you want me to have one, too?"

"You'll never settle down with one guy," Jessie said.

"Eventually I will," Lisa said. "I just want to try them all out *first.* That's why Friday nights are so important. Tonight, some of the kids are going to have a big bonfire on the beach. I was thinking of wearing orange to match the flames."

"Hold on, Lisa," Jessie said. "Don't you remember what tonight is?"

A look of horror crossed Lisa's pretty face. "Oh, no! Don't tell me I forgot a sale at the mall!"

"It's our first meeting of the Palisades Historical Society," Jessie said. "How could you forget?"

"I tried really, really hard," Lisa said in a small voice.

"Lisa, it was an honor to get a membership in the society," Kelly reminded her. "You came in first in the Palisades Historical Society Scavenger Hunt."

"Not to mention winning five hundred smackers," Zack said.

Jessie blushed, and Slater looked away. *Oops.* Zack winced. Kelly gave him a look that said he deserved five hundred *smacks.* He'd forgotten for a minute that the five-hundred-dollar prize was still a sensitive topic for Jessie and Slater.

Jessie had won the contest when she'd drained the oil out of Slater's car. She'd only done it because she'd thought that he was playing dirty. What she hadn't known was that not only hadn't Slater been cheating, he'd also had a faulty oil light. He'd burned out his engine before he'd realized anything was happening. Jessie and Lisa had given him the prize money to make up for it, but Jessie had been hurt when Slater hadn't exactly been appreciative of their gesture. In fact, he hadn't unbent one bit. He'd even broken up with Jessie the next day.

Jessie had made the mistake of telling Slater that she hadn't *owed* him the money or anything.

Then Slater had blown up and given her back the money. Jessie had tried to give it back to him again, but he wouldn't take it. Now he was working at Zero Zambezzi's garage to pay for the damage to his car.

Kelly rushed in to change the subject. She couldn't stand it when there were bad feelings in the gang.

"Well, I'm looking forward to my class," she said. "I can't wait to meet my instructor."

Lisa clutched her heart. "That curly hair. That crooked smile. Those muscles . . ."

Slater grinned. "Hey, Lisa, I didn't know you cared."

"I'm talking about Jamie Dolan," Lisa said, swatting at Slater's muscular arm. "I can't believe he's teaching Kelly's course. Are you sure you don't need a ride?" she asked Kelly.

"I borrowed my mother's car," Kelly said.

"Looks like you're stuck with me and the Palisades Historical Society," Jessie told Lisa.

"Who knows," Kelly said. "Maybe there'll be a cute guy there."

Lisa gave her a withering look. "Kelly, Kelly, Kelly. Get real. Cute boys and stuffy old historical societies just don't mix. Ever."

"Well, I'm looking forward to tonight," Jessie said enthusiastically. "Maybe we'll have a discussion about the role of Palisades in the Bear Flag Revolt. Or if there were any battles nearby during the Mexican-American War. Or gosh, how about the evolution of zoning laws. That can be really fascinating . . . Lisa?"

Lisa frantically waved her hands in the air. "Negative images," she puffed.

Just then, Derrick Weber strolled by. Lisa had been trying to make meaningful eye contact with him for months. He looked at her, startled, and waved back. Then, he paused at the stairs and fiddled with his backpack, as though he were waiting for her to catch up.

Lisa broke into a dazzling smile and started off after him. Jessie grabbed the tail of her turquoise linen blazer. "No way, girlfriend," she said.

"But Derrick is waiting for me!" Lisa wailed.

"So are the members of the historical society," Jessie said firmly.

"Gee, talk about negative images," Lisa grumbled. "I can see it now. I'll have to wave so hard at the meeting, I'll probably take right off."

Chapter 2

▼ ▲ ▼ ▲ ▼

Kelly threw her faded jeans back onto her bed and slipped into her brand-new pair again. She turned around in front of her mother.

"Well?"

"Oh, definitely those," Mrs. Kapowski said.

Kelly looked in the mirror and sighed. "It looks like I'm trying too hard." She wiggled out of the new jeans and fished through the pile of clothing on the bed until she found her black jeans. She quickly put them on.

"Now, those are smashing," her mother said.

"Too la-di-da," Kelly said with a sigh. "Like I'm trying to look hipper than I am." She picked up her faded jeans again. "Really, Mom. What do you think? I have to look perfect!"

Mrs. Kapowski sighed and stood up. "Kelly, I think I'm too old for this. Jeans are jeans, and you look pretty in all of them."

"But, Mom, I can't look like a dweeb or a nerd or a nobody. The outfit is *crucial.*"

"I think I'm going to have to limit your seeing Lisa Turtle to twice a week," her mother said in mock exasperation. Then she smiled. "Look, honey. If you want my advice, I'd say choose the outfit that makes you feel the most comfortable. The most you. And that's my last word on the subject."

Her mother closed Kelly's bedroom door softly. That was the trouble with parental advice, Kelly thought. It only made sense halfway. The problem was, there were a bunch of Kelly Kapowskis. She was shy and extroverted and serious and lighthearted all at the same time. Which side of her did she want to project tonight?

"The faded jeans," Kelly muttered. "Definitely. I think."

But she didn't have any more time to change. Kelly pulled her faded jeans back on, grabbed her car keys, and ran downstairs. She kissed her parents good-bye.

"I think you should have picked the black jeans," her brother Kirby said with a smirk.

"Oooooh, the corduroys, definitely," Kerry said. "They're so *you.*"

"Mmmmm," Kyle said. "I always go for plaid. It goes with everything."

"Eat some paste, you guys," Kelly said, dashing out the door. Sometimes it was death having three older brothers.

The ride to Los Angeles seemed to take no time at all. She found a parking space right in front of the building where the acting school was housed. Kelly wiped her damp palms on her jeans. She was so nervous! She hoped that in the first class she'd just have to listen. She'd die if she had to get up in front of everybody!

"Don't be a wimp, Kapowski," she muttered, opening the car door.

She found the classroom easily. It had a banked row of chairs that looked down on a small stage. Kelly climbed up the stairs until she found a seat in the second-to-last row.

She shyly peeked at the rest of the class. Everyone looked older than she was—and very self-assured.

"Hey, Molly," a blond-haired guy called. He was tall and overweight, with a friendly, open face. "Did you go to the go-see with Weinstock?"

The pretty girl with red curly hair shook her head. "Couldn't. I had a callback for *Yesterday's Child.* How about you, Peter?"

The guy shrugged. "I went. They saw. We'll see. Maybe I need new headshots. Maybe I need a new *face.*"

A striking girl with black hair and light green eyes tossed her overstuffed leather tote on a seat in the first row. She called over to the other side of the room. "Hey, Josh, did you hear? Larry got picked up by ICM. Can you stand it?"

An intense-looking guy with liquid brown eyes drew a finger across his throat. "Just kill me and get it over with, Dorian," he said. "That guy gets all the breaks. I hate him."

"Just 'cause he's cuter than you," Molly, the redheaded girl, teased.

Kelly looked at her shoes. She felt completely out of place. She had no idea what anybody was talking about. Callbacks. Go-sees. ICM. What was that, a supersonic missile?

She thought this was a *beginning* actors' class. Everyone talked like they'd been in the business for years. She was going to make a complete fool of herself.

Maybe she could leave. They'd probably give her a refund if she got a doctor's note that said she needed an operation or something. Or she could say she had to leave the country. Something. Anything. Because there was no way she could stay here and be humiliated in front of Molly and Josh and Dorian and Peter. Not to mention Jamie Dolan!

She was reaching for her purse when the door opened and a thin girl with glasses and a clipboard walked to the center of the stage. When she opened her mouth, Kelly was surprised to hear a rich, husky voice emerge.

"Can I have your attention, please?"

The class quieted. "I have some good news, some bad news, and some gossip hot off the presses," the girl said, and the class groaned.

"I'm sensing trouble," Josh said.

"Jamie Dolan has been hired to replace Alex Roman in Mervin Berlinger's new film," the girl said. "It's shooting in London, and he's on his way there tonight. And if you get to the phone quick enough, you can beat out 'Entertainment Tonight' and tell all your friends."

Dismay flooded Kelly. She wouldn't get to study with Jamie Dolan! Now that she *couldn't,* she wanted to so badly!

Josh groaned in disgust. "This isn't fair, Betsy," he said. "I went into hock to pay for this class."

"Anyone who wants a refund can get one," Betsy said. She pushed her glasses up her nose. "But before you decide, I—"

Josh stood up. "I can't believe Jamie Dolan

blew us off," he said. "I thought he was a professional. He made a *commitment.*"

"Like you'd turn down a chance to work with Mervin Berlinger," Dorian said dryly.

The class murmured agreement. Mervin Berlinger had won three Oscars for best director. He was able to get the strongest performances out of his actors.

"If you'd all just wait a second," Betsy said, "you'll hear the good news. Replacing Jamie Dolan will be the actor who made such a splash in *One Man's Story.* He's agreed to step in at the last minute. You all know Mitchell Tobias."

Kelly gasped, but her response was drowned out by the satisfied murmurs of the class. Mitch! She thought she'd never see him again. But there he was, striding through the door, as handsome and cocky as ever. She remembered every detail of their time together in New York City. But now he was practically famous. Would Mitch remember her?

▼ ▲ ▼

Lisa stifled a yawn. Then another. But finally, one sneaked through. Jessie poked her hard in the side.

"Stay awake," Jessie whispered.

Yeah, right, Lisa thought. *I'm going to stay awake for Mrs. Claude Culpepper's paper about some guy who kicked the bucket practically a hundred years ago.*

She'd much rather daydream about Derrick Weber instead. She'd been making eye contact with him for *weeks,* and today was the first sign that he was interested at all. Slowly, her eyelids began to droop.

Jessie poked her again.

Who was Mrs. Culpepper talking about? Lisa furrowed her brow and tried to listen. Wesley Racine. Right. The only thing Lisa knew about Wesley Racine was that he'd managed to get a zillion things named after him in Palisades. There was the Racine Opera House and Wesley Racine Middle School and the Racine Shopping Center—now *that* she could appreciate. Lisa even lived a block off Racine Avenue. As a matter of fact, didn't Lisa hear *enough* about the mighty Racines? Now Mrs. Culpepper even wanted to name a day after him.

"I have to see his name all over town," she muttered to Jessie. "Do I have to listen to a boring lecture about him, too?"

"Shhhh," Jessie said as Mrs. Culpepper announced that Wesley's wife, Amanda, had started the first library in Palisades.

"Whoop-de-do," Lisa said under her breath.

She squirmed over in her seat so that Jessie couldn't poke her again.

"And now I'd like to introduce the youngest member of the Racine family," Mrs. Culpepper said. "He's an honors student at Stansbury University—and a member of the historical society as well. I'm sure you all know Thomas Jefferson Racine."

Lisa stifled another yawn. But just then, a tall guy she hadn't noticed arose from an armchair in a shadowy corner. He went to the front of the room as applause broke out.

"Please, Mrs. Culpepper," a deep, amused voice said. "Call me Jeff."

Slowly, Lisa sat up. He was gorgeous! He had dark brown hair streaked with gold. She couldn't see what color his eyes were, but she liked how they sparkled. And that smile! She wanted to melt right off her chair into a puddle at Thomas Jefferson Racine's feet.

"Thank you for your presentation, Mrs. Culpepper," Jeff Racine said. "But I'm afraid I have to point out a factual error."

Mrs. Culpepper gave a flustered look at her notes. "Oh, dear, I worked so hard—"

"I'm no longer the youngest member of the Racine family," Jeff said with a smile. "My sister

Amelia had a baby last month. And my niece, if she could talk, would join the whole family in thanking you for proposing Wesley Racine Day for the town of Palisades."

The members of the society chuckled. Lisa laughed a little too loudly, and Jessie looked at her quizzically. Lisa leaned forward in her chair. Now, exactly what color were Jeff's eyes?

Mrs. Culpepper stood up. "May I see a show of hands of those who would like to join the committee to establish Wesley Racine Day in Palisades? We need to make the proposal to the city council, and there's plenty of work to do before then."

Lisa's hand shot in the air. Jessie gave her a puzzled look. What was Lisa up to? She'd been practically falling asleep during the whole meeting. Now she looked like the historical society's biggest booster!

"Ah, one of our newest members, Lisa Turtle," Mrs. Culpepper said. "Thank you for volunteering so quickly, Lisa."

"You're welcome, Mrs. Culpepper," Lisa said. "I think it's our duty as historians and citizens to establish Wesley Racine Day."

"What are you doing, Lisa?" Jessie whispered. "Why are you volunteering to be on some stuffy old committee? Even *I* don't want to research Wesley Racine."

"Amber," Lisa said dreamily.

"The name is Jessie," Jessie said. "Are you daydreaming again? Or are you asleep? That's the only way you could have volunteered for that committee."

"Jeff's eyes," Lisa said. "Some might call them brown. But, no. Definitely amber."

"Oh, no," Jessie said. "Don't tell me. Not another crush. Please. Anything but that."

Lisa sighed. "Did you see the way he smiled at me?"

Jessie began waving her hands in front of Lisa's face frantically. "No. Not again. I'm not over your last crush. Lisa, unrequited love is a *negative* thought. It'll give you wrinkles!" She waved and waved, trying to get the negative thought out of Lisa's head.

"Ah, Miss Spano is volunteering as well!" Mrs. Culpepper said. "And so enthusiastically, too!"

Chapter 3

▼ ▲ ▼ ▲ ▼

Kelly watched as Mitch Tobias spoke to Betsy, the administrator. She'd first met Mitch when she'd jumped into his cab in New York. She'd been impressed with his ambition and determination to make it. Of course, she hadn't been exactly immune to his looks, either. She'd come awfully close to falling for him, big time.

But Mitch lived in New York and she lived in California, and besides, she was going steady with Zack. Gradually, the memory of Mitch had faded. But when he'd made a huge splash in *One Man's Story,* Kelly had bought every magazine he'd been in and gone to see the film four times.

Maybe she still had a tiny crush on him. Or

maybe she'd just been impressed that he'd done exactly what he'd set out to do. He'd starred on Broadway and then gone on to Hollywood.

Betsy left, closing the door softly behind her, and Mitch faced the class. "I know you're all disappointed that Jamie won't be teaching the class," he said. "But I'd ask you to do me a favor. Stay for the first class. Then, if anyone wants a refund, Betsy will be available."

Mitch thrust his hands into his pockets. "First, I'd like to give you a short version of my résumé. I went to Juilliard, and I've studied with some of the best acting teachers in New York."

Mitch reeled off the names of teachers Kelly had never heard of. Most of the rest of the class nodded in recognition. Even Josh looked impressed.

"Okay," Mitch said easily. "Now I'd like to hear about you—why you're here, if you've done any acting. Would you like to start?" he said to Dorian.

Mitch went around the room, listening intently to each student. Kelly's palms got damp. What was she going to say? Should she remind Mitch of their meeting? Since she was in the back, it seemed to take forever until Mitch got to her. His electric blue eyes rested on her without recognition.

Kelly's heart fell. She couldn't help feeling disappointed. Obviously, their meeting had meant a lot more to her than to him. And he'd said that he'd never forget her!

But then, Mitch did a double take. He looked right into her eyes and grinned. "Hey, California!" he said.

▼ ▲ ▼

"Again," Mitch said to the class. They were all standing in a circle on the stage.

"Ma-may-me-mo-mu," Kelly said along with the others. She felt completely silly, but nobody else looked the least bit embarrassed.

"Dang-a-dang-dang-dang-didley-dang-a-dang-dang-dang-do," she sang. According to Mitch, she was limbering up her mouth, lips, and tongue. According to her, she was making a fool of herself.

"Okay, everybody, roar," Mitch said. "Big like a lion."

"RRRRRRROOOOOOAAAARRRRR," Kelly heard Josh growl next to her.

"rrrrrrroar," she said.

"More, Kelly," Mitch said.

"Rrrrrooooar," Kelly tried.

"Better. Okay, now, people. Let's bring it down. Tiny, tiny, tiny, like a mouse."

"eeeeeeeee," Josh said.

This is acting? Kelly thought. *It's more like a day in the life of Screech.*

"Now let's get serious," Mitch said.

Great, Kelly thought. Now they'd really get started. What would Mitch start with? Shakespeare? Shaw? Chekhov?

"Let's pretend we're all walking on Jell-O," Mitch said.

▼ ▲ ▼

After class, Kelly was thrilled when Mitch invited her out for something to eat. He took her to a little café down the street from the school.

"I didn't know if you'd remember me," Kelly admitted as she tasted her piece of chocolate mousse cake. She almost had to pinch herself to make sure she wasn't dreaming. This had been her fantasy when she visited New York. She'd pictured herself studying to be an actress, sitting in cafés, and talking about plays and movies and acting. The dream had always revolved around Mitch.

"How could I forget you?" Mitch asked. "You were my good luck charm, remember? Because of you, I got to meet Max Springer. He gave me my first break."

"I didn't really have anything to do with it," Kelly said, blushing. "It was Screech. He's the one who introduced you."

"But I wouldn't have known your friend if I hadn't known you. And you were the one who was so nice to me. You believed in me," Mitch said. He covered her hand with his. "Back then, that meant a lot."

"It was easy," Kelly said.

Mitch withdrew his hand to pick up his coffee, and Kelly felt a tiny spurt of disappointment.

"So how did you like the class?" Mitch asked.

"It was great, but . . ." Kelly shook her head, laughing. "I didn't realize that acting could be so embarrassing."

"Acting exercises can be weird, at first," Mitch agreed. "But it's all about loosening up. Not being afraid to be in front of people."

"I just hope that impersonating a strip of bacon cooking won't be my greatest role," Kelly said, and Mitch laughed. "I can't wait to really *act*, though," she added. "I really want to be good."

"I'll help you as much as I can," Mitch promised. He took a sip of coffee. "So," he said casually, "do you still have that boyfriend?"

"Yes," Kelly admitted. "Zack and I are still going steady."

Going steady. It suddenly sounded so childish. Kelly wished she had said "seeing each other." Going steady sounded so . . . high school.

But Mitch didn't give her a condescending look. He just nodded and took another sip of coffee. He looked kind of disappointed.

But the awful thing was that Kelly was, too.

▼ ▲ ▼

Lisa picked up Jessie bright and early Saturday morning. "Isn't it a beautiful day?" she called through the car window as Jessie came down the walk.

"Gorgeous," Jessie grumbled. "That's why we should be spending it at the beach. Not the library."

"We can go for a late-afternoon swim if we have time," Lisa said as Jessie slid into the front seat. "But I don't think we will. We have a lot of research to do. We have to present a really strong case to the society so they'll vote for Wesley Racine Day. Then we move on to the city council."

"I'd like to declare Jessie's Beach Day instead," Jessie said, pulling the brim of her baseball cap down and scrunching up in her seat as Lisa took off. She yawned. "I don't want to have to write a paper on Wesley Racine. I write enough papers in school."

"Lighten up," Lisa said. Her dark brown eyes were shining. "It'll be fun."

Jessie let out a snort. "Can you believe this role reversal, Lisa? I want to go to the beach, and you're dragging me to the library."

Lisa couldn't help giggling. "Never would have guessed it, girl."

Jessie sighed and looked out the window. "I wanted to scope out Slater at the beach today, too. He's probably going to be showing off his muscles to all the girls. What a jerk."

"But you wish he was still *your* jerk," Lisa pointed out.

"True," Jessie admitted.

Lisa coasted to a stop at a red light. "I owe you one, Jess. I admit it. If you'll just do me this favor and help me with this paper, I'll be in debt to you for the rest of my life."

"You said it," Jessie agreed.

"I just know this is the way to get Jeff's attention," Lisa said. "I think he's going to ask me out. Did you notice how he smiled when I volunteered? And after the meeting, didn't he ask me if I wanted a second glass of punch?"

"He also got a plate of cookies for Mrs. Culpepper," Jessie pointed out. "Does that mean he's going to ask *her* out, too?"

"Don't be negative," Lisa said. "I can't wave the thoughts away—I'm driving."

For the rest of Saturday, the two girls

researched early Palisades history at the library. They had to ask the librarian for special access to old records and a rare edition of *The Palisades I Love*, by Wesley's son, Patrick Henry Racine.

Lisa found out fascinating facts about Wesley Racine. After the city was incorporated in 1858, Wesley was its first mayor. He was the head of the volunteer fire department and helped put out the fires that almost destroyed Palisades after an earthquake. His wife brought the first touring opera company to town. They owned the largest ranch for miles around. Wesley even ran for governor once, but he lost.

At one o'clock, Jessie started to droop, and Lisa told her she could go. Jessie grabbed her beach bag and headed the few blocks to Palisades Beach, hoping to catch a glimpse of Slater. Lisa kept on working.

She pictured herself reading a glowing tribute to the city council. Jeff would be there. His amber eyes would be aglow as he gazed at her. He'd come up afterward and take her hand. . . .

I never realized what an incredible researcher you are, Lisa. Those facts! Those dates! Those conclusions! I'd be honored to take you to dinner.

She would get the guy using brains and good study habits, Lisa thought, chewing on her pencil. She grinned. Now *that* would be a first, for sure.

Loaded down with books on early California history, Lisa staggered to her car. She drove home, trying to decide what to wear to the next historical society meeting. It was weeks away, but it was never too early to plan. Maybe she needed a totally new outfit. Everything she had was so frivolous—hot pinks and yellows and oranges. Something in tweed might be good. Sure, it was eighty degrees out, but the town hall was air-conditioned.

When she opened the front door of the house, the phone was ringing. Lisa snatched it up breathlessly and said hello.

"Lisa? This is Jefferson Racine."

Jeff. Lisa dropped the books, and they fell to the floor with a thud.

"Uh, Lisa? Are you there?"

"I'm here."

"What was that, thunder? It doesn't look like rain."

"It was a bunch of books. I dropped them. I just got back from the library." *Lisa, relax. You sound like a robot.* She took a deep breath. Jeff had called her! She'd never worked *this* fast before.

"Wow, you really take the research stuff seriously," Jeff said. "You've already started."

"Oh, I do," Lisa said. "I really think your great-great-grandfather was incredible."

"Actually, I think he was my great-great-*great-*

grandfather. Listen, that's why I'm calling. I just had a brainstorm and I thought I'd run it by you."

"Run away, Jefferson," Lisa said. *Or, actually, run this way.*

"Call me Jeff. Jefferson sounds so . . . presidential."

Lisa laughed. "All the Racines have those intimidating names. I guess Wesley started the tradition with his son. Patrick Henry Racine. Then there was Benjamin Franklin Racine. And isn't your grandfather James Madison Racine? It's a lot of name to carry around."

"Tell me about it," Jeff said. "I think I'll name my son something like John Wilkes Booth Racine. Now *that* would shock my grandfather."

"Especially since your father's name is Abraham Lincoln Racine," Lisa said with a giggle. "So what's your brainstorm, Jeff?"

"Well, we keep a lot of old family papers and documents right here in the house," Jeff said. "My ancestors saved *everything.* It's all cataloged, too. If you'd like, you could come over tomorrow or some evening next week and look through the family archives. It would save you having to plow through all those history books."

"I'd love to," Lisa breathed. It wasn't a date. But it *almost* was! Maybe the invitation was just a way to see her again. "Tomorrow's fine."

"Great," Jeff said. "How about eleven o'clock?"

"I'll be there," Lisa promised. She never dreamed she'd look forward to going through musty old papers on a sunny Sunday. But with Jeff Racine at her side, it sounded like the most romantic date in the world.

Chapter 4

▼ ▲ ▼ ▲ ▼

"Okay, people," Mitch said on Saturday morning. "Before we get to scene study, we're going to warm up with some trust exercises. For those of you who are beginning actors, these exercises are to show you that every actor onstage is important, no matter what his or her role. You rely on each other, and you have to trust each other. First, we'll try the push-me-pull-you exercise."

Beside her, Kelly heard Lynette, a six-foot-tall brunette, moan. "I hate this one," she whispered.

"What is it?" Kelly whispered back. Whatever it was, she didn't know if she *wanted* to trust some of these people.

Lynette didn't get a chance to answer. Mitch called them forward and had them form a circle.

Mitch asked Josh to demonstrate. Josh crossed his arms and then simply fell toward Peter, on his left. Peter caught him and tossed him to Dorian, who pushed him over to Alex. Josh was pushed around the circle. When he got to Kelly, she was surprised at the deadweight. Josh wasn't trying to save himself from falling. He was just trusting that she'd be able to catch him.

When it was her turn, Kelly found the exercise harder than she'd thought. She couldn't loosen up her body enough. Some part of her was afraid that Josh or Peter wouldn't be able to catch her.

"Loosen up, Kelly. Trust your fellow actors," Mitch urged. Kelly tried to be loose. But all she felt was awkward. How could she trust people she wasn't even sure she *liked*?

At least she was the last person to go. Maybe she'd learn to trust everyone later.

"Okay," Mitch said. "Now let's do body lifts."

Body lifts?

"Uh-oh," Peter said, looking down at his round stomach. "Anybody got a crane?"

The rest of the group laughed. Kelly hoped that body lifts weren't what she thought they were.

But they were. A few minutes later, Kelly found herself lying down in the middle of the circle. Everyone took a part of her—an arm, a foot, her head—and lifted her slowly until she was over their heads. Kelly lay rigid, her eyes closed, and prayed they wouldn't drop her. Would she get a refund? Maybe she'd just break an ankle or a wrist. Or a finger. She'd sacrifice a finger or two to be an actress. . . .

Mitch sounded stern this time. "Kelly, relax!"

She tried to relax. She tried as hard as she could. But she just got more nervous. She was relieved when Mitch instructed the class to lower her back down.

Even though she wasn't exactly a pro at the trust exercises, Kelly looked forward to scene study. She didn't even mind when Mitch paired her with Josh for her first reading. Josh was the most experienced actor in the class.

Mitch gave them a scene from a contemporary play called *Dreamin' on L Street.* It had been a big hit Off Broadway the year before. Kelly's character was a tough girl named Toni. Josh played her boyfriend.

Kelly read through the scene. It took place the morning after Toni has stayed out all night wandering the streets. Her boyfriend, Benny, confronts her. The emotions swing crazily from anger to defiance to hurt to affection and back to anger again. Kelly couldn't believe Mitch had picked this for her first scene!

First, Mitch had them read through the scene

out loud. Then they put the script down and ad-libbed the scene from what they could remember, concentrating on the emotions of their character. That was hard. But then Mitch asked them to do the scene without saying a word! That was hardest of all.

Finally, they did the scene as written. Then Mitch gave them feedback and they started again. Mitch was so patient and helpful that Kelly almost lost her self-consciousness.

For the first time, Kelly saw that Josh was kind of arrogant for a reason. He was good! He was totally believable as Benny. Sometimes she believed him so much she was scared he was going to explode. Then she remembered that she was supposed to be Toni.

Kelly had no idea whether she was good or not. By the time Mitch let them sit down, she felt like she'd run a marathon.

After class, Kelly waited until the rest of the students had filed out. Then she approached Mitch shyly. "It was a great class," she said. "Thanks for being so patient with me."

"You did fine, Kelly," Mitch said. "Don't look so depressed."

"I don't know about those trust exercises," Kelly said. "I don't know how to trust people I don't know. I'm not even sure I like some of them."

Mitch laughed. "I know what you mean. But

I'm not asking you to like every actor you work with. Maybe this is the only time in your life that trust *isn't* based on liking someone. It's based on respecting them as professionals."

"I see what you mean," Kelly said. "I guess I have a lot to learn. But the thing is . . ." Kelly faltered, embarrassed. She wanted to ask Mitch a favor. But she didn't want to impose on him.

Mitch stuffed a towel into his leather backpack. "What is it, Kelly?"

"There's this talent contest at school," Kelly said in a rush. "I'd really like to enter it and do a dramatic monologue. But I don't know if I'm ready."

"Why don't you work on a monologue from the play I assigned you today?" Mitch said. "I'll show you which one. Lots of actresses use it for auditions."

"That would be great," Kelly said. "But the thing is, the contest is only two weeks away, and . . ."

Kelly saw Mitch glance at his watch. "I know you're busy," she said quickly. "I'd better get going."

"No, no," Mitch said. "I do have to stop by my agent's office, though. Listen, why don't you come with me? We can talk on the way. Do you have time?"

"Sure," Kelly said. Was Mitch kidding? It would be totally thrilling to go to the office of a real Hollywood agent.

They drove to his agent's office in Mitch's car, a sporty yellow convertible. "I wanted red, green, blue—anything but yellow," Mitch said with a grin. "After driving a cab in New York, I was sick of the color. But the leasing company only had this one available."

"I like it," Kelly said. "I just hope there isn't a meter running."

Mitch laughed. "I won't even ask for a tip," he teased.

Mitch's agent, Murray Posner, was part of a large agency that handled big stars. The agency had a whole building in downtown L.A., a huge skyscraper that gleamed with polished granite and smoked glass. As Mitch guided her into the chrome-and-marble lobby, she looked down at her jeans in dismay. "I feel kind of underdressed," she said.

"That's one of the good things about this profession," Mitch said. "You don't need an expensive wardrobe. Don't sweat it, Kelly. Murray's a workaholic. Most normal people don't work on Saturdays. Besides, you look great."

Mitch always made her *feel* great, Kelly thought. It wasn't that he lavished compliments on her. He just had a way of saying the right thing at the right time. And he really *noticed* her. She and Zack had been together so long that sometimes she wondered if he really looked at her anymore at all.

"Murray is a great guy," Mitch said as they went up in the elevator. "He was the best agent in New York. Then he got this incredible offer and moved out here. He makes me feel at home. L.A. is kind of scary sometimes. Murray and I both miss New York. We can sit around and talk about delis and pizzerias for hours."

Murray was on the phone when his secretary led them into his office. He waved at them with a stubby hand and indicated that they should sit down. Then, when he was finished with one conversation, he switched to another line.

"I haven't found anybody yet," he said tersely into the phone. "I have some calls out. I'm *sure* I can find you the perfect girl. No, Vicki wouldn't do it. She's a vegetarian. I *told* her you'd use tofu for the shoot. She's allergic to soybeans. Okay, okay. I'll call you back."

He hung up the phone and let his bald head drop into his hands. "Why me?"

"What's the matter, Murray?" Mitch asked. "Problems?"

"Of *course* I have problems," Murray said woefully. "I'm an agent; it comes with the territory, along with an ulcer. Uncle Sam's Hamburg Haven is shooting a commercial in three days and Gigi Hoffman canceled on me. The casting agent is torturing me, he calls me every five minutes—hey, who's she?" Suddenly Murray pointed at Kelly.

"This is a student of mine, Kelly Kapowski," Mitch said. "Kelly, this disgruntled gentleman is Murray Posner."

"How do you do, Mr.—," Kelly started.

"Can she act?" Murray asked, staring at her. He waved his hand. "Doesn't matter. You just have a couple lines." He peered at her. "Are you a vegetarian?"

"No," Kelly said. "Actually, I love Uncle Sam's hamburgers. I eat there a lot."

"Perfect," Murray said. "You want to try out for a commercial?"

"Me?" Kelly squeaked. "I don't have much experience."

Murray waved a hand. "It's okay, kid. If Mitch recommends you, you're okay by me. Besides, I'm desperate. Can you go for the audition right now?"

Kelly hesitated.

"I can drive you," Mitch said.

"Yeah, Mitch can drive you," Murray said. "What do you say, Kathy?"

"Kelly," Mitch said.

"Kelly," Murray said. "I'm sorry, I'm losing my mind here. What do you say? Want to audition?"

"I-I guess so," Kelly stammered.

"Terrific. You can get the address from Barbara on the way out. Call me afterward, tell me how it was. Okay?"

"Okay," Kelly said.

"Mitch, we'll talk later. I didn't get the contracts yet, anyway." Murray waved at them. "Tell Barbara to order me a bagel on your way out, will you? Not that they know from a decent bagel in L.A. I miss Seventh Avenue."

"Tell me about it," Mitch agreed.

"Bye, now. Break a leg, Kelly. Lightly toasted. The bagel, I mean." Murray picked up the phone again and was already talking as they closed the door.

Kelly found herself whizzing down an elevator, clutching a piece of paper with a strange address in her hand. She felt dizzy and scared, but somehow it was a good feeling. She was heading to her first audition!

Chapter 5

▼ ▲ ▼ ▲ ▼

On Sunday morning, Lisa couldn't find anything the least bit studious in her wardrobe, so she borrowed a vest from her dad and wore it with her jeans. Somehow, the pinstripes made her pink silk blouse look more serious.

Lisa followed Jeff's directions and headed out of town. She drove onto a winding road that meandered through the golden hills east of Palisades. Jeff had told her to look for a pair of Spanish iron gates. He'd leave them open for her. Lisa followed the road until she saw some massive iron gates that she guessed looked Spanish. She turned onto a long drive lined with eucalyptus trees. She cranked down the window farther so she could smell their perfume.

The road cut through a stand of pine trees, and then Lisa saw the Racine house. She gulped. Mansion was more like it. It was a huge, rambling stucco home with a red tile roof. When she peered through the tall trees shading the west wing, Lisa could see the glint of a pool in the back.

She parked the car and rang the bell alongside the wide oak door. She heard footsteps, and Jeff opened the door. His smile made her heart do a fast hip-hop dance in her chest.

"Lisa! Welcome," he said, stepping aside.

Lisa stepped into the coolness of the tiled hall. "Your house is beautiful," she said.

"Thank you," Jeff said. "Wesley built the original structure way back in the eighteen forties. It was only three rooms. Then after he bought the surrounding land, he added another wing. Every generation has added something since. Let me take you to the study."

Lisa caught glimpses of beautiful, formal rooms as Jeff led the way to the rear of the house. When he opened the study door, she gasped in surprise. The windows revealed an incredible view over the hills. Her eyes traveled from the sparkling pool with its brightly colored chaise lounges, past the green trees down to the city of Palisades sprawled below. Beyond the city, she could even see the Pacific.

"I didn't realize we were up so high," she said.

"It's a great view, isn't it?" Jeff said. "I never get tired of it. You should see it at sunset."

Lisa had a sudden picture of Jeff and her, sipping iced teas by the pool and watching an orange ball slip over the rim of the dark water. It was in her future, she just knew it.

"I'm sure it's wonderful," she said.

"Here are the papers I was talking about," Jeff said. "I left them on the desk. You'll see that they're cataloged. Some of the papers are over a hundred years old. Oh, that reminds me. I have to ask you not to take any of the papers out of the house. They're just too valuable to my family."

"Of course I won't take anything," Lisa assured him. "And I'll be super careful."

"Lisa, I just want to say thank you again," Jeff said. He looked down and then away. "It's weird growing up a Racine in Palisades. I mean, I see our name everywhere. It's kind of awkward."

"I guess it might be," Lisa said. "I always thought it would be neat. But I do see what you mean."

"When they call the roll at school or on a team, everybody looks at you. I really hated that when I was a kid. I almost hated the name Racine. But now I'm proud of what my family has done. I'm not embarrassed to admit it."

"I think your family should be honored in Palisades," Lisa told him. "That's why I volunteered for the committee."

Jeff's amber eyes were warm as he smiled at her. "We all appreciate it. My grandfather hasn't been this excited in years."

Lisa smiled back. She couldn't wait to sit beside him, their heads together, sifting through history, maybe making a little of their own. . . .

"Well, I'll leave you to it," Jeff said.

Leave me to it?

"Susana, our housekeeper, left a couple of sodas and some sandwiches for you. If you need anything, you can use the house phone. Just press *kitchen.* And if you want me, just ask Susana. She'll find me. I'm going to go riding for a while, but I should be back in an hour or so."

"I'm sure I'll do fine," Lisa assured him. But she couldn't help feeling a little forlorn. This wasn't a date, after all. She would hardly get to see Jeff.

But after Jeff left and she sat down at the big oak desk, Lisa soon became engrossed in her task. So this was how historians worked, Lisa mused, turning over the yellowed sheets of paper. They read letters and birth certificates, tax notices and land titles, and they pieced together a story. Some of the papers she couldn't figure out, and some were just dull. But as she read, she slowly put together the details of Wesley Racine's life and times.

She stopped to eat a delicate ham sandwich and have a cola, and then went back to work. Later in the afternoon, Susana knocked softly and put a plate of cookies by her elbow. Lisa munched on them while she went over her notes. She sipped another cola by the window, looking at the view. Then she went back to work again. She'd never dreamed going through musty files could be so fascinating.

Despite the colas, Lisa began to yawn by midafternoon. Maybe it was time to wind it up, she thought, lazily opening an old ledger book. The endpaper was a beautiful tortoise design, but Lisa saw a tiny sliver of yellow. She fingered it and discovered that a piece of paper was lodged behind the endpaper of the ledger.

Lisa's heart beat a little faster as she carefully peeled back the endpaper and slid out the hidden paper.

The paper was so old, it felt as soft as a piece of suede. Carefully, slowly, she unfolded it. Her eye traveled over the old-fashioned language written in faded ink.

Lisa frowned. It couldn't be.

She read it again. Something tolled in her brain, a phrase here, a word there, a name.

Could it really be true?

She reached for a stack of Amanda Racine's old letters and began to search.

▼ ▲ ▼

On Monday morning, Kelly couldn't wait for Zack to pick her up for school. She waited outside her house, hugging her books. When he pulled up, she ran excitedly toward his Mustang.

"I got a part!" she sang out as she ran toward him.

Zack leaned out of the window. "What did you say? You got a wart?"

"A *part,*" Kelly said. "An acting role."

"Already?" Zack asked.

Kelly opened the door and got in. "I tried to call you all day yesterday," she said.

"I was helping my father at the new offices. They don't have phones yet," Zack explained. "How did you get a part? And for what?"

"It's for a TV commercial," Kelly said, her deep blue eyes shining. "For Uncle Sam's Hamburg Haven. It's only four lines, but still—I'll be on TV!"

"That's fantastic, Kelly! I'm so proud of you. How did it happen?" Zack asked as he pulled out of the driveway.

"I went to see Mitch's agent with him, and he sent me over," Kelly explained happily.

Zack scowled. He hadn't been very happy when Kelly had told him that the great Mitchell Tobias would be teaching her seminar. Even though they'd never talked about it, he suspected that Kelly still harbored a tiny crush on the handsome actor. That guy was just too good-looking. Zack had felt a lot more comfortable when Mitch was three thousand miles away.

But his resentment melted when he looked over at Kelly. She was so thrilled. He couldn't spoil her mood.

"You must have done really well at the audition," he said.

Kelly giggled. "Actually, I didn't. I flubbed my lines three times. I was so nervous! But I lucked out. Sam Zeiderman was there—Uncle Sam himself. Apparently, I look like his daughter. He had the director give me another chance. Then they all huddled together for a while. Finally, the director came back and told me I was in!"

"I'm really impressed, Kelly," Zack said. He reached over and squeezed her hand quickly. "And I'm very proud of you. You're quite talented."

"How do you know? You haven't seen me act yet," Kelly said with a grin.

"So what? I already *know* you're a star," Zack insisted. "You've got charisma."

Kelly hesitated. "As a matter of fact, Zack, I

want to ask you a favor. I've decided to do a monologue in the talent contest. I worked on it all day yesterday and tried to remember all of Mitch's advice from class. But I'd really like you to tell me what you think."

"I'd be glad to, Kelly," Zack said. "I'm sure you're fantastic."

"I'll talk to Ms. McCracken and see if I can use the stage during our free period today," Kelly said. "Would you come and give me some feedback? And you have to be honest, Zack. You can't lie to spare my feelings. Really. All criticism is constructive, Mitch says. You just have to remove your ego from the performance."

Now you're quoting the mighty Mitch? Zack wanted to say. But he only smiled. "Of course," he said. "But I won't have to lie. I know you'll be terrific."

▼ ▲ ▼

Kelly stood in the middle of the bare stage. "So I'm tellin' you," she said, "I'm gonna make it. Not because I'm good. Not because I'm pretty or smart. I'm not any of those things. I'm gonna make it because nobody thinks I can. Maybe that's not a good reason. But it works for me."

Zack put his hand over his mouth and coughed to conceal a snort of laughter. He couldn't help it.

The sight of Kelly trying to talk tough was just so . . . funny.

What was he going to do? Kelly was a terrible actress. Her delivery was wooden. Her movements were stiff. She was totally unbelievable as Toni. Put everything all together, and you got comedy, not drama. And Zack knew that this play wasn't supposed to be a comedy.

"So I'll be movin' out, Pop," Kelly said flatly, as if she was talking about doing the laundry. "If you ever happen to notice I'm gone, wish me well."

It was over, thank goodness. Zack wiped his forehead. It had been the longest five minutes of his life.

Kelly stepped forward. She peered into the first row. "Well, Zack? How was it? Remember, you can tell me the truth."

Kelly looked at him eagerly. Zack cleared his throat. He'd promised to be honest. He'd sworn he'd tell her the truth.

"You were fantastic," he lied.

"Honest?" Kelly squealed.

"Honest," Zack said, a smile frozen on his face. He just couldn't tell her she stunk. She was his girlfriend. She was the love of his life. He couldn't hurt her like that.

But if she went onstage next week, she'd be

the laughingstock of Bayside High. *Somebody* had to tell her. As long as it wasn't him.

Jessie. She didn't have a dishonest bone in her body. And she was tactful, too. She was the perfect person to tell Kelly. She would be gentle and kind and honest. If anyone could do it, Jessie could.

Chapter 6

▼ ▲ ▼ ▲ ▼

"She can't be *that* bad," Jessie said.

Zack shrugged.

"She is?"

He nodded.

"But—"

Zack shook his head.

"Gosh," Jessie said.

Slowly, Jessie sank down on the flowered couch in the Morris living room. She was on her way to meet Lisa, but Zack had called and begged her to stop by for only five minutes. Since his house was right next door, Jessie had run over before getting into her car.

"I'm counting on you, Jess," Zack said desperately. "You've got to tell her. She'll be humiliated.

You know how Kelly hates for people to laugh at her."

"Okay," Jessie said. "I promise I'll give her my honest reaction. Now I have to run. Lisa is all freaked out for some reason."

"Uh-oh," Zack said. "Something serious?"

"Probably just boy trouble again," Jessie said. "She's being super mysterious. Look, I'll talk to Kelly tomorrow."

"You're a pal," Zack said. "Remember: be kind."

"She can't be *that* bad," Jessie said again.

Zack sighed. "Gosh," Jessie muttered. She grabbed her purse and headed out the door.

She ran back across the lawn to her driveway and started up her car. Lisa had asked her to come to the Palisades pier, and it was only a short drive up the coast. Jessie found a space, parked, and then walked down the pier all the way to the end, where some fishermen were trying their luck.

The pier was a strange place for Lisa to pick to meet. It was a gloomy, overcast day, and it was chilly on the water. The souvenir stands were empty of the tourists who usually bought T-shirts and caps with LIFE'S A BEACH written on them. Lisa had called the pier tacky plenty of times. Besides, she hated the smell of fish.

But she was waiting at the end rail for Jessie,

staring out to sea. She was wearing sunglasses and a hat with a brim that shaded her face.

"Haven't you noticed, Lisa? There's no sun today," Jessie said as she came up to her friend at the railing. "As a matter of fact, I think it's starting to rain."

"Shhhh," Lisa said. "Keep your voice down." She looked around nervously. "I don't want anyone to hear what we're talking about."

"What *are* we talking about?"

"Shhhhh!"

"Okay, okay," Jessie said in a low tone. "What is it?"

"I found something out at Jeff's house," Lisa said darkly. "Something horrible about the Racine family."

"The *Racines*?" Jessie blurted.

"Shhhhhh!" Lisa looked around carefully. "This is top secret, Jess! I was looking through this old ledger and found a letter concealed inside it. Someone must have hidden it there. It was a letter from this guy Javier Salazar to Wesley Racine. Javier Salazar used to own the Racine land. The letter was written in eighteen fifty-one."

"Wait a second. Wesley bought his land from this guy Salazar?" Jessie asked. "So what?"

Lisa shook her head. "Wesley didn't buy it. He

stole it from Salazar," she said. "Salazar was of Mexican descent. Remember when we studied early California history? Most of the state was Spanish-speaking until the gold rush. That's when all the American settlers poured in. Wesley didn't make money in the gold rush, Jessie. He didn't *have* any money when he moved to Palisades. So he just . . . took some land. He was able to swindle the land title from Salazar."

"Oh, my gosh," Jessie said. "Are you sure?"

"The letter was from Salazar asking Wesley to act honorably and give him back the title," Lisa explained. "When I read that, I went back to a reference in one of Amanda's letters. She says something about the Salazar family going back to Mexico and how it makes it easier not to see them in town anymore. I thought Salazar was just someone who *worked* for Wesley. But I can see now why Amanda didn't like looking at the family. He had four daughters. One of them was only four years old! And they had to go back to Mexico without anything, Jessie!"

"This is awful," Jessie breathed.

"The Salazars had a big ranch," Lisa explained. "They had cattle and horses and workers. And they'd owned the land for generations. Wesley took all their property and livestock. He just *took* it."

"This is unbelievable," Jessie said. "What did you tell Jeff?"

Lisa sighed. "I didn't tell him anything. I just said I had to spend some more time digging and I'd come back this week. I have to gather more facts. I need more proof. What if Salazar was lying?"

"It doesn't sound like it," Jessie said dubiously.

"But he *could* have been," Lisa insisted. "Anyway, I just couldn't tell Jeff. He's so proud of his family. He'd be crushed."

Jessie looked out over the water and sighed. "Maybe he already knows, Lisa. The Racines *have* to know. Somebody hid that letter, after all."

"No way," Lisa said. "Not Jeff."

Jessie looked at her sharply. "How can you be so sure?"

"I just am," Lisa said. "Someone like Jeff couldn't know. He's too good, and nice, and down-to-earth—"

"And cute," Jessie said irritably. "Honestly, Lisa. Sometimes your boy craziness is just plain crazy."

"What are you talking about?" Lisa asked.

"You don't even *know* Jeff," Jessie said, exasperated. "He refilled your punch glass Friday night, and on Sunday you exchanged about three sentences."

"But—"

"There're no buts, Lisa," Jessie said. "Look, let's not get sidetracked. The important thing is to document your suspicions and present them to the historical society. We owe it to them. It would be super embarrassing if they pushed Wesley Racine Day to the city council and then this information came out later."

"That's true," Lisa said. "Poor Jeff!"

"This issue is bigger than Jeff Racine," Jessie snapped. "This is about truth and justice and the city of Palisades."

There goes Jessie on her soapbox again, Lisa thought. Give the girl a cause, and she was ready to fight. Lisa knew she had to find out more facts, but she knew something else: there was no way she'd let Jessie embarrass Jeff and his family.

▼ ▲ ▼

On Tuesday afternoon, Kelly felt like a complete professional as she drove to the shoot. She had gotten time off from school, and the gang had been jealous. Zack had joked that she'd do *anything* to get out of chemistry lab.

There weren't just butterflies in her stomach. There were caterpillars, too. She opened the door to the Uncle Sam's Hamburg Haven they had chosen for the location. She stepped over cables and around cameras until she found the assistant director. He brought her to makeup and wardrobe. Kelly was fussed over and pushed into five different outfits until they settled on jeans that were exactly like the ones she was wearing, and a white T-shirt with red, white, and blue suspenders. Then she went to the director.

"Did you study the script and the camera directions?" he asked her. "You know what to do?"

Kelly nodded. "I'm letter-perfect." It wasn't hard to be. She only had four lines.

For the first shot, all she had to do was turn away from the counter with a tray full of food and smile. Then, for the second shot, she had to hold up the cheeseburger and say, "I'm a true-blue American. And I love Uncle Sam! Don't hold the pickles!" Then she was supposed to bite into the cheeseburger and say, "Mmmmm."

Kelly had no problem with the first shot. She'd done so much modeling that it was a cinch to smile into a camera, even while balancing a tray.

But when she got to the second shot, Kelly discovered that her nerves were back. She took several deep breaths to center herself while the cameraman lined her up in the viewfinder.

"Ma-may-me-mo-mu," she said under her breath. "Ma-may-me-mo-mu."

The director, Charlie Fox, poked his head around the camera. "Uh, Kelly? Did you say something?"

"I'm just warming up my chords," Kelly answered.

"It ain't Shakespeare, kid," Charlie Fox said.

Kelly blushed. She felt even more nervous now. They thought she was an amateur!

"Okay. Quiet on the set," the assistant director called.

"Remember, Kelly, you're about to eat your very favorite cheeseburger in the whole wide world," Charlie Fox told her. "You want this cheeseburger more than world peace. Got it, sweetheart?"

"Got it," Kelly said.

"Action," Charlie Fox said, and pointed at Kelly.

"I'm a blue-true American—," Kelly began.

"Cut," Charlie Fox called.

"I'm sorry," Kelly said, flustered. "I just got mixed up."

"It's okay," he said patiently. "Take a deep breath and start over."

Kelly took a deep breath. Charlie Fox called, "Action."

Kelly smiled. "I'm a true-blue American. And I love—" What did she love? Kelly blinked. She couldn't remember her line. "I love Uncle Sam!" she blurted out.

"Cut," Charlie Fox called. "One more time, Kelly. Concentrate."

Action!

"I'm a true-blue American," Kelly said. "And I love Uncle Sam! Don't hold the mayo!"

▼ ▲ ▼

Charlie finally called a halt at seven o'clock. Kelly put her head down in her arms. She felt hot and exhausted and faintly nauseated from having taken thirty-seven bites of a cheeseburger. She had been able to spit out most of the bites, but her mouth tasted like mustard and onions and pickles. If this was acting, she should take up ditchdigging to get some rest.

She felt a friendly hand rest briefly on top of her head. Kelly raised her head. Mitch stood next to her, smiling.

"Hi," she said. "Did you come to scrape me off the floor and put me back together?"

He laughed. "Tough day?"

"Try working up enthusiasm for a cheeseburger after thirty-seven takes," Kelly said.

Mitch looked uneasy. "You did thirty-seven takes?"

"Is that bad?" Kelly asked. "You told me that sometimes you have to do take after take to get it right."

"Of course," Mitch said quickly. "I'm sure everything went fine."

"I flubbed my lines a couple of times in the beginning," Kelly said, rising wearily. "But then I was perfect. I don't understand why Charlie kept yelling 'more, more' at me, though."

"He probably wanted you to project," Mitch said.

"Project what?" Kelly asked.

Mitch shrugged. "Enthusiasm. Excitement. Whatever."

"I did," Kelly said. "But I don't even *like* pickles."

Mitch laughed and slung an arm around her shoulder. "It sounds like a typical first shoot to me. I know just how you feel. Once I had to put down a tray of dog food for this awful-smelling pooch fifty-nine times. Something kept going wrong."

"Really?" Kelly asked. "That makes me feel a teeny bit better. I wish I hadn't blown the first couple of takes. I was so nervous!"

"Listen, I'll tell you what," Mitch said. "Why don't we go grab a bite, and I'll tell you some relaxation techniques to calm your nerves before a shoot."

"Just tell me one thing," Kelly said. "Does it involve impersonating a vacuum cleaner again?"

Mitch laughed. "If you don't behave, young lady, that bite you grab is going to be a—"

"Cheeseburger," Kelly and Mitch said together.

Chapter 7

▼ ▲ ▼ ▲ ▼

"Gosh, after yesterday, I'm a little nervous about this," Kelly said to Jessie the next morning at school. They were sitting in the first row of the auditorium, where Jessie had agreed to watch Kelly's monologue. "I'm afraid I'll forget my lines."

"Don't worry about it," Jessie told her. "It's only me."

Kelly gestured at the stage, her face alight. "I just love the theater, Jess," she said. "Deciding to become an actress was the best decision of my life. I think I've finally found something I'm good at besides cheerleading. I mean, I know I *can* be good, if I work at it. Mitch believes in me."

"Ah," Jessie said.

"Don't say 'Ah' that way," Kelly said. "Mitch and I are friends."

Jessie smiled. "Ahhh."

"We have a professional relationship," Kelly said primly.

"Ahhhhh," Jessie said. She waggled her eyebrows at Kelly and giggled.

Kelly couldn't help laughing. "I asked you to give me feedback, not torture me," she said.

Jessie put her hands in her lap and a serious expression on her face. "Okay. The judges are ready."

Kelly went up the steps to the stage. She kept her back to Jessie and closed her eyes to gather her concentration. Then she turned around and began the scene.

Kelly didn't forget a line—or even a word. But Jessie watched her, stunned. Zack was right. She *was* awful! Jessie didn't believe Kelly's transformation into a tough-talking teen for one second. As a matter of fact, sometimes Kelly was almost . . . funny. Jessie put a hand over her mouth to hide a smile. Then she coughed to disguise a giggle.

Finally, Kelly finished. She stepped forward a few steps. "Well?"

How could Jessie burst her bubble? Jessie had been the one to encourage Kelly to start acting lessons in the first place. How could she tell Kelly to forget it?

But she'd promised Zack, as well as Kelly, to tell the truth.

"Jessie? Was I okay? Be honest, now."

Jessie took a deep breath. "You were fabulous," she lied.

She just couldn't tell Kelly the truth. She wasn't the right person to do it. *Slater* was. He was Mr. Blunt. But he could tell you the awful truth and then make you laugh about it. He'd treat you to a pizza and tell you stories about all the times he had messed up or acted like a jerk. Yes, if anybody could do it, Slater could.

▼ ▲ ▼

That afternoon, Lisa drove with Jessie to the Racine house. Jeff had given them permission to do more research in the family archives. He said he had late classes that day, but that Susana would let them in.

Lisa rang the bell while Jessie tapped her foot impatiently. "Why do you have to look like you're going to war?" Lisa whispered to Jessie.

"Sometimes finding out the truth *is* war," Jessie said, her hazel eyes flashing.

The door opened. To Lisa's surprise, an old man with white hair stood there. He was leaning on a cane and looked frail. But his amber eyes were warm and friendly. Lisa knew instantly who he was.

"You must be Jeff's grandfather," she said. "I'm Lisa Turtle and this is Jessie Spano."

"The girls from the historical society," James Madison Racine said. "But I didn't expect you to be so young and pretty. What are you girls doing going through musty old records? You should be out having fun." His eyes twinkled. "I wish I still could."

"I bet you manage," Lisa replied, grinning.

He laughed. "I can see why my grandson has been singing your praises, Ms. Turtle. Come in, please. I can't tell you how gratified the family is that the society is interested in sponsoring a Wesley Racine Day."

"He was an important figure in Palisades history," Lisa said nervously. *How can I hurt this nice old man?* she thought.

"He was a cranky old coot," James Madison Racine said. "At least, that's what my grandfather told me. Now follow me."

Mr. Racine led them to the study. "Well, I'll leave you two alone," he said. "Susana is going to bring you in some tea and cookies at four."

As soon as the door closed behind Mr. Racine, Lisa collapsed onto the overstuffed leather sofa. "They're so *nice,*" she moaned. "Maybe we'll find out that Salazar was the crook."

"I wouldn't bet on it," Jessie said, sitting down at the desk. "Now let's get to work."

▼ ▲ ▼

The teapot sat cooling and the homemade cookies lay untouched on the plate. There was no way Lisa and Jessie could accept the Racines' hospitality when they might have to expose their terrible secret.

The two girls sat slumped on the couch, watching the shadows on the golden hills.

"I guess there's no mistake," Lisa said with a sigh. "Wesley *did* swindle the ranch from Salazar."

"And without remorse," Jessie said. "Not only was he a crook, he was a bigot. He thought Mexicans were subhuman." She shuddered. "He was an awful man."

"His wife was the one who did all the good in Palisades," Lisa mused. "Maybe we should have an Amanda Racine Day. But even she put up with Wesley's prejudice and his swindles."

"She had to," Jessie said. "You can tell she liked being rich."

"You know what really got me?" Lisa asked. "When Wesley was mayor, he proposed that law to run all Mexicans out of town. Can you imagine?"

"And it almost passed," Jessie said with a deep sigh. "Then his grandson Benjamin Franklin

Racine supported that law that if any Mexican was caught without papers, he or she could be driven right over the border and dumped there."

"Wesley passed his prejudice down along with his money," Lisa said.

"There's no way that Palisades can set aside a day to honor this man," Jessie said, waving at the papers in front of them. "Not only because of all the Mexicans in town, but for *all* of the people. It would be wrong."

"I agree," Lisa said. "But I don't think the whole town has to know what kind of a man he was. There's no reason to embarrass the Racines that way."

Jessie frowned. "I guess not. But we *do* have to tell the historical society."

"And Jeff," Lisa said gloomily.

"The thing is," Jessie said, "we need documentation."

Lisa looked at her. "Documentation? What are you getting at?"

"The only evidence we have is right here," Jessie said, tapping the papers. "What if the Racines decide to say we're mistaken? We can't prove anything."

"The Racines wouldn't do that," Lisa said.

Jessie raised an eyebrow at her. "Lisa, look at

the evidence. They're a bunch of unprincipled, prejudiced . . . bad guys."

"But that was *before,*" Lisa said. "A hundred years ago. That doesn't mean that Jeff's parents or his grandfather are bad."

"Maybe not," Jessie said. "But we still have to be able to back up what we're saying. We have to smuggle some of these papers out of the house."

Lisa sat up, horrified. "We can't, Jessie," she said. "I promised Jeff I wouldn't remove anything."

"Lisa, we don't have a choice," Jessie said fervently. "Don't you see? They could deny everything if we don't have proof. They could destroy the records. We *have* to have evidence."

Lisa sat back, stumped. She knew that Jessie was right. But she didn't want to break her promise to Jeff.

"Well, *you* didn't promise not to take anything," she said slowly. "So if you happened to slip a few papers into my satchel, it wouldn't be like *I* broke a promise."

"Right," Jessie said. She gathered up several sheets of paper and placed them carefully in one of Lisa's textbooks. Then she slipped the book back into Lisa's leather satchel.

"I didn't see that," Lisa said, resolutely looking out the window.

"Don't worry, Lisa," Jessie said. "We can find a way to slip the papers back after we copy them."

"I think we should tell Jeff before the meeting next week," Lisa said. "It would be mean to surprise him."

Jessie nodded. "I agree. Do you want to do it?"

"No way, girlfriend," Lisa said with a sigh. "But I will."

▼ ▲ ▼

"Well, Slater?" Kelly asked eagerly. "How was I?"

Slater shuffled his feet. When Jessie had asked him to do this, he'd thought she'd been exaggerating, as usual. But she'd been right on the money. Kelly was a terrible actress. When, as Toni, she demanded respect, it was like she was asking for a pinker shade of nail polish. He'd started to guffaw and then had faked a coughing fit to cover it.

"Slater?"

He'd promised Jessie to tell Kelly the truth. But it wasn't like Jessie hadn't broken promises to him. Promises to be honest with him. Promises not to fly off the handle all the time. Promises to trust him, for once. That curly-headed, acid-tongued, irritating, gorgeous pile of trouble had broken all her promises the day she'd sabotaged his car so she could win the Palisades Historical Society Scavenger Hunt.

"Was I okay?" Kelly asked.

Slater tore his thoughts away from his ex-girlfriend and looked at Kelly. She was so sweet. She didn't have a mean bone in her body. He was too much of a gentleman to hurt her. Then again, she'd be hurt even worse if she did this monologue in the talent show. And he *had* promised her to be honest.

"You were terrific, momma," he lied.

Kelly glowed. "Really?"

"Totally awesome," Slater said.

"Thanks, Slater," Kelly said happily. "You're a pal. And take care of that cold. I heard you coughing all through my performance. You must have caught a cold from Jessie. Or Zack."

Kelly gathered up her books and went off happily. Slater sighed. He'd ask Lisa to tell Kelly the truth, he decided. Lisa always shot from the hip. If anyone could tell Kelly, Lisa could.

▼ ▲ ▼

"Why me, Slater?" Lisa asked wearily. She twisted the phone cord in her fingers. "I have enough problems with the truth these days. Don't make me do this, too."

"It's Jessie's fault," Slater said. "She was supposed to be honest with Kelly, and she couldn't do it."

"Come off it, Slater," Lisa said. "Nobody wants to tell Kelly the truth. You've all been passing the buck." She sighed. "Okay, I'll do it. I'll ask Kelly to do her monologue for me tomorrow."

She hung up the phone and rested her chin in her hands. How could she tell her best girlfriend that she stunk *and* her hopefully soon-to-be boyfriend that his family was rotten, all in the very same day? It was too much for anybody to handle. Maybe she could get sick. Just a little sick, just enough so that she could stay in bed with pillows behind her head and watch soap operas all day. Then she could forget about the soap opera waiting for her tomorrow.

Lisa felt her forehead, but she wasn't feverish. Her throat wasn't even the teensiest bit sore. It looked like she'd have to get up tomorrow after all.

Beside her, the phone shrilled, and Lisa let out a groan. Was there someone else's heart she had to break tomorrow? It rang again, and she snatched it up. She was positive that she was about to develop her very first migraine headache.

"Hello?" she said.

"Lisa, it's Jeff Racine."

"Jeff! Hi," Lisa chirped. She was so surprised

to hear his voice that she sounded like a chipmunk. She cleared her throat and tried to speak in a low, sexy tone. "How are you?"

"Not very good. I have to ask you something," Jeff said. He sounded rushed and upset. "My grandfather went into the study after you left to look at some of Wesley's and his wife's old letters, and he's positive there're some papers missing. You didn't take them, did you?"

Lisa hesitated. She could say no, and it wouldn't be a lie, exactly. But it wouldn't be the truth, either. Why did everything have to be so complicated?

She sighed. "Yes," she said.

"Yes?" Jeff asked incredulously. "You did?"

"Sort of," Lisa said.

"But, Lisa, I asked you not to," Jeff said angrily. "Those papers are extremely fragile. I can't believe you'd just remove them!"

"I'm sorry, Jeff," Lisa said. "All I can say is that I had a good reason."

"I'm waiting," Jeff said.

Lisa twisted the phone cord around her finger until it hurt. "Can I tell you in person?" she asked. "I really don't want to go into it on the phone."

"I guess so," Jeff said.

"Can you meet me tomorrow afternoon at around four-thirty?" Lisa asked.

Jeff blew out a long breath. "Okay."

Lisa told him the name of a café in town, and he wrote down the address. "I won't tell my grandfather about this yet," he said. "I'll see you tomorrow."

"Tomorrow," Lisa said. She hung up. When she'd dreamed about her first date with Jeff Racine, she hadn't expected it to involve deceit and accusations.

Lisa groaned and flopped back on the pillows. She was *definitely* getting her first migraine.

Chapter 8

▼ ▲ ▼ ▲ ▼

When Kelly arrived at the shoot that afternoon, Charlie Fox called her over.

"We've decided to change the focus of the commercial, Kelly," he told her. "We're going for action rather than dialogue. We want a more dynamic feel, you know?"

Kelly nodded. "Okay. What would you like me to do?"

"Well, you've been doing just fine, sweetheart. A fabulous job. What I want you to do today is really put a lot of oomph into the 'Mmmmm.'"

"Ooomph into the 'Mmmmm,'" Kelly repeated, nodding. "Got it. What about my lines? Are we going to change them?"

"We're going to drop them," Charlie said.

"Drop them?" Kelly asked, disappointed.

"I really think the 'Mmmmm' says it all, don't you?" Charlie asked. He patted her on the arm. "Put everything you've got into that 'Mmmmm.' Keep that same fabulousness and add some ooomph. Got it, sweetheart?"

"Got it," Kelly said. She was disappointed that her lines were cut. But as Mitch would say, that was show biz.

Today, the shoot went much easier. In fact, it only took nine takes. Finally, Charlie called out, "Print," and Kelly's very first professional acting job was over.

When the lights were switched off, she saw Murray sipping a container of coffee behind the cameras. She waved to him and went over.

"Thought I'd come and see how you were doing, kid," he said.

"It went better today," Kelly said.

"Heard they cut your lines," Murray said.

"Charlie wanted a more dynamic feel," Kelly explained. "So I just had one line."

"Mmmm," Murray said.

"That was it!" Kelly said with a nod.

"No, I meant, 'I see,'" Murray said.

"You see what?" Kelly said, looking around.

"Nothing, kid." Murray made a face. "They make terrible coffee here. No wonder they need commercials. You taste the coffee, you never come back. Listen, Kelly, the reason I came by was because I think I've got another audition for you."

"Another one? Already?" Kelly said excitedly. "Wow. I mean, okay, sure. What is it for?" She modified her tone so that she sounded crisp and professional.

"A sitcom."

"A sitcom?" Kelly squealed. She threw her arms around Murray and jumped up and down. "Oh, my gosh!"

"Hey, you're spilling my terrible coffee. Calm down. It's just an audition, kid. I didn't say you had the job." Murray's tone was gruff, but he smiled as he handed her a manila envelope. "Here are your lines. It's a small part, but it's funny. It might get you noticed. I thought I'd drop by, to see how you do."

"When is it?" Kelly asked, fingering the envelope.

"Tomorrow afternoon, two o'clock, Continental Studios."

"Continental Studios," Kelly breathed. It sounded so . . . Hollywood.

"So can you get off from school okay?"

"Absolutely," Kelly said, nodding. "I just have to skip last period." She'd call Mr. Belding tonight. He'd been totally impressed that she got a commercial. He'd even asked her for Meryl Streep's autograph. Mr. Belding would definitely let her miss last period as long as she made up the work.

Murray raised a tired finger. "See you there, kid." He ambled off.

Kelly slipped the pages out of the envelope and scanned them quickly. This time, she'd prepare on her own. She wanted to surprise Mitch. Wait until she told him she had a real part!

▼ ▲ ▼

Lisa nervously headed for the café she'd picked for her meeting with Jeff. She desperately hoped that when the time came, she would find the right words to tell him what she'd discovered.

She'd already struck out today with Kelly. When push came to shove, she couldn't tell Kelly the truth. So she'd lied and told Kelly she was fantastic.

Screech would have to tell Kelly, Lisa decided. He was absolutely incapable of deceiving anybody. They should have asked him to do it in the first place.

Jeff was already waiting when she arrived. He was sitting in a corner booth, sipping on a soda and reading one of his textbooks. He looked up and frowned when Lisa slid into the booth across from him.

"Did you find the place okay?" Lisa asked.

He nodded. "No problem."

"They have good salads and sandwiches here," Lisa said. Her voice trailed off at the end as Jeff looked impatient. If only she could discuss food all afternoon! *You simply must try the shrimp salad on a toasted onion bun, Jeff. Oh, and did I mention that your ancestor was a bigot?*

Well, she might as well begin.

"The reason Jessie and I took the documents, Jeff," Lisa said, "is that we found something in them. Something I don't think you're going to like hearing. We discovered something about Wesley Racine. . . ."

▼ ▲ ▼

"You don't believe me," Lisa said flatly a few minutes later.

Jeff shook his head slowly. "It's not that," he said. "It's just . . . well, it's a lot to take in."

"I'm truly sorry, Jeff," Lisa said gently.

"It's not your fault," Jeff said distractedly.

Lisa twirled the straw in her soda. "The thing is," she said, "you can see why Jessie and I can't support Wesley Racine Day. And we're going to have to tell the historical society what we learned."

Jeff ran a hand through his sun-streaked hair. "I guess," he said. He sat thinking a moment. "Wait a second, Lisa. Let's look at this. Sure,

Wesley Racine was prejudiced. But he was a man of his time. Why should that overshadow all the good things he did for Palisades?"

"Like trying to run the Mexicans out of town?" Lisa asked dryly.

"Lisa, I'm not trying to excuse that," Jeff said, a stricken look on his face. "It makes me sick. But there wouldn't *be* a Palisades without Wesley Racine."

"I'm not so sure about that, Jeff," Lisa said. "And what good does it do to talk about what might have been? We have to deal with what *is*."

"Look," Jeff said, "I'm named after Thomas Jefferson. He's an American hero, right? A president, a scholar, an inventor—all those things. And he kept slaves. Sure, it was immoral. Terrible. But that was what southern gentlemen like him did back then. Does that cancel out all his accomplishments?"

Lisa shook her head. "It's not the same thing."

"But it is!" Jeff said. "Don't you see that?"

"Jeff, in case you haven't noticed, I'm African American," Lisa said. "Prejudice isn't just some abstract thing to me. It's something that my ancestors have been fighting against for generations and generations. And I can't give my support to a man who practiced it so cruelly. No matter how many opera houses he built." Lisa's voice shook at the end, and her eyes filled with tears.

Jeff didn't say anything for a minute. Then he reached over and covered her hand with his. "You're right," he said. "And I'm sorry. I was talking like a jerk. It's just that, all my life, I've been told what a great person Wesley Racine was. I was trying to excuse him."

She shook her head as she felt a tear slide down her cheek. "It's okay, Jeff. I understand—"

"No, it isn't really okay. I shouldn't have been so defensive. But now I see you're right."

Lisa sniffed. Jeff's hand felt good covering her own. She felt closer to him than ever.

"Can you do one thing for me, Lisa?" Jeff asked suddenly.

"Sure," Lisa said. "I mean, I think I owe you."

"Can you let me be the one to withdraw the proposal for Wesley Racine Day next week?"

Lisa nodded. "Of course. Whatever you want."

"And will you and Jessie keep mum about the reason why? Not for me," he said quickly. "For my grandfather. He's so frail, Lisa. The family history is practically all he has left. He wants to write a history of the Racine heritage and leave it for me and my sister. He's been messing around with those papers for months. Of course, I know his version will be totally bogus now. But it's really important to him. It's what he's living for. I just can't hurt him like that."

Lisa sighed. She'd reached her quota this week for blowing things open with the truth. Jeff was probably right. It was better to just let it be.

"All right, Jeff," she said. "Jessie and I won't say anything."

"Thank you. And could you give me back the papers you took?" Jeff asked. "Grandfather knows the letters aren't complete. He'll be asking for them."

Lisa hesitated for a second. She hadn't had a chance to copy the papers yet. But now there was no reason to. Jeff was going to withdraw the proposal himself. She reached into her satchel and handed the papers over to Jeff.

Their fingers touched, and he smiled. "Oh, and one more thing," he said softly. "What are you doing tomorrow night?"

Chapter 9

▼ ▲ ▼ ▲ ▼

"You did *what*?" Jessie said.

"I gave him back the papers. He's going to withdraw the proposal for Wesley Racine Day," Lisa said. "I *told* you."

"I know you *told* me," Jessie said, impatiently pushing back a lock of hair. "I just wasn't sure I heard right."

Lisa closed her locker door with a bang. "I don't know why you're so upset, Jessie. After all, the papers did belong to Jeff's family. How could I refuse to hand them back?"

"Simple," Jessie said. "Stall. Say you didn't have them. You probably didn't even *hesitate*."

"Why should I have?" Lisa countered. "Jeff completely understood. I sat there, trashing his family, and he was able to be objective. He's wonderful," she said mistily. Then she turned back to Jessie angrily. "And you're making him sound like a criminal!"

Jessie narrowed her eyes and inspected Lisa's shining eyes and flushed cheeks. "Hold it a second," she said. "Just tell me one thing. Did he ask you for a date?"

Lisa nodded happily. "Well, yes. We're going out tonight. He's taking me to that new Thai place by the beach."

"You hate Thai food," Jessie said.

"Not really," Lisa said. She sighed. "I can't wait!"

Jessie stamped her foot. "Lisa, how can you be so stupid! If you had half a brain, it would have nobody to play with up there. Don't you see what Jeff did? He conned you. He pretended to agree with everything you said. Then in order to get the papers back, he asked you out!"

"He did not!" Lisa protested. "He asked me out *after* I gave him the papers."

Jessie snorted. "So? He was clinching the deal. That was the bribe. You keep your mouth shut. He'll wine and dine you for a couple of weeks until it all blows over."

Lisa was so angry she wanted to explode. She

tried to count to ten, but she only made it to three. "How dare you, Jessie Spano," she said in a low tone that shook with fury. "What you're saying is a complete insult. First of all, is it so weird that a guy like Jeff Racine would be interested in me? And second of all, am I so stupid that I would swallow whatever somebody says? You're not giving me any credit."

Jessie sighed. "Of course I don't think you're stupid, Lisa. You've got a mind like a steel trap. But as soon as boys are involved, it gets covered in marshmallow goo."

"You weren't there," Lisa said stubbornly. "You don't know how sincere Jeff was."

"Tell me something, Lisa," Jessie said. "If Jeff agrees with us, why does he want us to keep our mouths shut at the historical society? What if he's going to maneuver behind our backs?"

"He's worried about his grandfather," Lisa said. "You saw how frail he was. He's a sweet old guy. The only thing he has left is his family pride. We can't destroy his faith in his family's good name."

"Is that what Jeff said?" Jessie asked scornfully.

"What's wrong with that? I think it's totally sweet that he wants to protect his grandfather," Lisa said.

"Excuse me?" Jessie said. "Protect James Madison Racine, one of the worst exploiters of migrant workers in the valley? Back in the sixties, he broke a strike with goons and baseball bats. And in the seventies, when the cancer rate among workers was thirty times higher than the national average due to pesticides, he tried to bribe a government worker to suppress the statistics. He's just continuing the family tradition!"

Lisa felt weak. She leaned back against her locker. "He did all that?"

Jessie nodded. "While you were handing over our proof on a silver platter, I was doing more research on the Racines."

"I don't care," Lisa said slowly. "I still don't think that Jeff is bad. I still believe in him."

"Lisa, you don't even *know* him!" Jessie cried, exasperated.

The bell rang, and Lisa hitched the strap of her satchel more firmly on her shoulder. "I'm going with my instincts," she said firmly. "Jeff Racine is a stand-up guy."

Jessie stared at her. She didn't know whether to strangle Lisa or try to knock some sense into her head. "Don't you see, Lisa?" she asked pleadingly. "When it comes to guys, you get swamped by emotion. You don't look at a situation realistically."

"Oh, really, Jessie?" Lisa asked coolly. "Well,

maybe if you followed your emotions when it came to guys, you'd still have a boyfriend."

Jessie gasped. She couldn't believe Lisa was saying such a mean thing to her. And the cruelest part of all was that it was *true.* Because she listened to her head, her overly logical, calculating *bone-head,* she'd lost Slater. If she'd listened to her heart, she would have known he wouldn't cheat. She wouldn't have lost him.

Lisa saw how deeply she'd hurt Jessie. She could have bitten her tongue in half. But her head was still ringing with Jessie calling her *stupid.* She was too angry to apologize.

"I have to get to class," Lisa mumbled, and walked away.

▼ ▲ ▼

Screech sat down in the first row of the auditorium. He put his knapsack on the seat next to him, adjusted a purple sock, and straightened one of his orange suspenders.

"Are you all set?" Kelly asked from the stage.

"All set, Kelly," Screech said, unwrapping his sandwich.

"Uh, Screech? I know I asked you to do this during lunch period and everything," Kelly said. "But would you mind not eating until I'm through? It really interferes with my concentration."

"Of course," Screech said. He rewrapped the sandwich and put it back into his plaid lunch box. "Now, break a neck."

"A leg, Screech," Kelly said. "That's what you say to actors instead of good luck."

"Break a neck *and* a leg?" Screech said. "Wow. You're going to end up in traction."

He settled back in his seat as Kelly gathered her concentration and then began the scene. She'd been working on it every night, and she'd added some gestures and a new emphasis on different words. Instead of starting off angry, she let the scene build the way Mitch had taught her. He'd gone through the whole speech with her, pointing out the possible beats, which were where an actor would decide to hesitate to add emotion.

Finally, Kelly finished. She took a few steps forward to peer into the first row.

"Well, Screech?" she asked. "You're the last one of the gang to see my monologue. What do you think?"

"Gosh, Kelly," Screech said. "Whew. I mean, I'm relieved. You weren't *that* bad."

Kelly's expectant smile froze on her face. "Excuse me?"

"Well, from the way Zack and Jessie and Slater and Lisa were talking, I thought you'd really stink up the joint. I don't think you'd be *humiliated* if you entered the talent contest. Maybe a little embarrassed. But I don't care what Zack said. Nobody is going to throw rotten tomatoes at you. Not even ripe ones, I don't think. I mean, I have an apple here in my lunch box, and I didn't even think about throwing it once. . . . Kelly? Is something wrong? Your face is starting to look like a ripe tomato—Kelly?"

Kelly stalked by Screech without a word. Her long, dark hair flying, she marched up the aisle of the auditorium.

Screech squirmed out of his chair. "Kelly?" Grabbing his lunch box and knapsack, he tripped over his own feet as he tried to hurry after her. "Kelly? Did I say something wrong?"

▼ ▲ ▼

Zack was just about to take his first bite of lasagna when he saw Kelly burst into the cafeteria. Her eyes moved down the tables until they found him.

"Uh-oh," he said.

"What is it, preppy?" Slater asked. "Is Mr. Belding hunting you down again?"

"What class did you cut this time, Zack?" Jessie asked, taking a bite of her sandwich.

Lisa giggled. "And what contagious disease did you say you had?"

Zack gulped. "It's not just me that's in trouble this time, gang."

Lisa twisted around and saw Kelly bearing down on them. "Oh, no," Lisa said. "Maybe I shouldn't have asked Screech to break the news to Kelly."

"You asked *who*?" Slater asked.

"Screech?" Zack asked. He slumped down in his chair. "We're sunk. Using Screech as a diplomat is like using Schwarzenegger as a wimp."

Jessie didn't say anything. She and Lisa weren't talking, and so Jessie didn't want to make matters worse by criticizing her. And now Kelly probably wouldn't be speaking to her, either. Jessie had lost both her best girlfriends in one week. That's what happened when you tried to tell the truth.

Kelly finally came up to their table. "Thanks a lot for talking behind my back," she burst out. "Screech told me what you've been saying. That I'm awful and I can't act and I'm going to humiliate myself." Kelly shook her head. "How *could* you? You're my best friends!"

"We couldn't tell you, Kelly," Zack said. "We didn't want to hurt your feelings."

"You were so happy being an actress," Jessie said.

"We didn't want to discourage you," Lisa said.

"We didn't want to hurt your feelings," Slater said. "That's all."

"So you talked about me behind my back?" Kelly said.

"We were just trying to decide what to do," Zack explained.

"Well, thanks for nothing," Kelly said, looking from one face to another. "Thanks for not believing in me. Thanks for not having faith in me."

"Of course we have faith in you," Zack said. "We just don't think . . . well, that you're a very good actress."

"Oh, really, Zack?" Kelly asked, her deep blue eyes flashing furiously. "Is that why I've already gotten an acting job? Is that why I have a Hollywood agent? Is that why I'm going to an audition for a sitcom this afternoon?"

"You are?" Jessie asked dubiously.

Kelly turned to her. "Hard to believe, isn't it? Especially since I'm such a bad actress."

"Gosh, Kelly, we didn't mean to cut you down," Lisa said. "Maybe it was the monologue. You just weren't very believable as a tough girl."

"Mitch thinks I'm good," Kelly said angrily. "Of course, he's only a famous professional actor. It's not like he knows more than you guys or anything."

Zack looked helplessly at the gang. What could they say? Kelly *had* been awful. But to her, it looked like they'd deliberately set out to hurt her.

"Kelly, we're just being honest," Zack tried gently.

"No, you're not," Kelly said, tossing her head. "You're being *jealous.* I'm practically a professional, and you just can't handle it."

"That's not it," Jessie said. "Why would we *want* you to be bad, Kelly?"

"Maybe because then you couldn't look down on me anymore," Kelly said. "Everybody is good at something except me. Screech has computers. Lisa has design. Slater has sports. Jessie has academics. And Zack has . . . has—"

"The record for school suspensions?" Slater suggested.

"Whatever," Kelly said. "You know what I mean."

"Kelly, you're good at lots of things," Jessie said. "Cheerleading, for one."

Kelly gave her a withering look. "And I know just how much you respect *that,* Jessie."

Jessie squirmed. Maybe she shouldn't have put down cheerleading as aerobic stupidity.

Zack stood up. "Kelly, it doesn't matter to us if you're good at one thing or plenty of things or nothing at all. You're the best person I know. We love you because you're you."

"That's all I'm good for," Kelly said. "Being *sweet.* I want something more than that! Can't you understand?"

"Of course we can," Lisa said.

Kelly shook her head. "No, you can't. Because if you could, you wouldn't have been so mean to me. Well, I'll tell you what. Just do me a favor. Save those rotten vegetables you were going to throw at me. You might want to eat them instead of eating your words! Because I'm going to be great. You'll see!"

Kelly stormed off. Slowly, Zack sank back down into his seat. "Well, we sure blew that one," he said.

Screech ran up to them, his lunch box banging against his leg. "I just saw Kelly," he said.

"We saw her, too, Screech," Zack said with a sigh.

"I don't know what you guys meant when you said she was terrible," Screech said, sitting down. "She really gets into her character. Just now, she told me to take a long walk off a short pier. I guess she's still in character as that Toni person. I think she's a really great actress!"

Chapter 10

▼ ▲ ▼ ▲ ▼

Kelly felt completely cool and collected at her audition. Somehow, the confrontation with Zack and the gang had strengthened her resolve. She was determined to show them she could do it.

The role in the sitcom was of a ditsy, scatter-brained freshman at college who's caught her boyfriend kissing another girl. As the guy gives her more and more outlandish reasons for being in a lip lock with a stranger, she swallows every one. Kelly had the part down cold. Hadn't she played this scene over and over with Zack?

When her name was called, Kelly faced the director and the producer confidently. She'd already had her first job. This should be a piece of cake. She saw Murray walk onto the set with his usual container of coffee. Good. She was glad her agent would see the audition.

She would even get to read with one of the stars of the show, Jeremy Vane. He ambled onto the set and smiled in a vague, friendly way at her.

If only the gang could see her, Kelly thought. She was reading with a real television star. Of course, everyone thought "Take a Break" was the lamest show ever. But it was still TV!

"Anytime you're ready, kids," the director called.

Jeremy Vane turned to her. "Brenda! It's you!"

Kelly answered with her line, and they played the scene together. She put everything she had into it. She had decided to use a baby voice for the role, and she hoped she was really funny.

In only minutes, the reading was over. Kelly waited for the director to say something. But he was staring down at a clipboard in his lap. Jeremy Vane only gave her another vague smile and a yawn, and then went back to his dressing room.

"Thank you, Miss Kapowski," the director finally said.

"Uh, is that it?" Kelly asked. She peered behind the lights. Didn't they want to talk to her?

"That's it."

"Oh," Kelly said.

"Miss Kapowski? Would you mind clearing the set?"

"Oh," Kelly said again. "Sure." She walked toward the director. "My agent is right over there," she said.

He looked up at her. "Good for you."

"Um, will there be a callback, or is this the final audition?" she asked.

"It's the final one," the man said. He blew out an exasperated breath. "Is this your first audition?"

"No," Kelly said quickly. "Well, it's my second," she admitted. "Was I okay?" she asked hesitantly.

"How old are you? Sixteen? Seventeen?" At Kelly's nod, the director sighed and passed a hand over his silver hair. "Listen, Miss . . . uh—"

"Kapowski."

He winced. "Right. Anyway, if I were you, I'd go back to school and stay there for a while. Act in some more school plays. Take some acting lessons."

"I don't understand," Kelly said. "Wasn't I any good?"

He looked back at his clipboard. "Don't quit your day job." He looked up and saw her expression. "Look. Some people have it, and some people don't. Don't waste my time and yours, okay?"

Kelly took a step backward, stunned. The casual cruelty of the comment shocked her. Until now, everyone had been so nice to her. This director was telling her that she stunk!

She turned on her heels and rushed across the studio. Blinded by tears, she almost ran into Murray.

"What's the matter, kid?" he asked softly.

"Th-that director . . . ," Kelly stammered. "He just practically told me to forget it."

Murray took a sip of coffee. "Ah."

"What do you think, Murray?" Kelly asked pleadingly. "Do you think I'm any good?"

Murray sighed. "Kelly, I like you a lot. But you've got a ways to go before you're a pro, okay? You're very pretty. The camera loves you. But you have to study more."

"You mean I stink."

"You just can't deliver a line, kid. You open your mouth and mush comes out. Look, I might as well tell you. The only reason you weren't fired from the commercial was because that Uncle Sam guy, the client, liked your looks. The director cut your lines because he couldn't get a performance out of you."

"So why did you send me here?" Kelly said in a shaky voice.

"Because I wanted to give you another chance," Murray said. This time, he sounded gentle instead of gruff. "And I wanted to see for myself. It could have been a lousy director the other day, someone who didn't have patience with you. But that's not it, Kelly." He gave her a kind look. "I blame myself. I pushed you too far too fast. You're not ready for a professional audition. You just started studying, for crying out loud. Now, don't look at me with those big blue eyes of yours. I've got a bad heart. You could break it."

Kelly smiled through her tears. "Thanks for being so nice, Murray."

"Yeah, well, don't tell anybody. Come on, I'll walk you out."

Murray tossed his coffee container into a trash can, and they headed for the door.

"I should have listened to Mitch," Murray said. "He told me you weren't ready for speaking roles. I pushed you—no question about it."

Kelly swallowed. Mitch had said that? But he'd been the one who'd been encouraging her! So he'd been lying all along! He thought she didn't have any talent, either. And he'd let her be completely humiliated! Somehow, that was the worst betrayal of all.

Murray left her at her car, told her to stay in touch, and got into his Mercedes. Kelly sat for a minute, trying to calm down. She didn't know if she felt more embarrassed or more angry at Mitch.

"Kelly!"

She heard his voice, and she turned. He strode across the parking lot toward her. She waited until he came up.

"How did the audition go?" Mitch asked, leaning into her open window.

"It went awful," Kelly said crisply. "I was terrible, and the director told me so pretty plainly. Then Murray added his two cents. But you're not very surprised, are you? Because you think I stink, too. I just don't know why you didn't tell me."

Mitch looked down at his hands. "Kelly, you just started acting. I didn't want to discourage you."

"But you could have been honest with me," Kelly said, her eyes filling with tears again. "Instead, you led me on."

Mitch shook his head. "I didn't see it that way. I was trying to encourage you. You're my student. And my friend, I hope."

"Friends don't lie to each other," Kelly said stonily.

"I didn't lie, Kelly. I was trying to help you," Mitch insisted.

"Well, it doesn't matter," Kelly said. "I know the truth now. And I'm going to quit the seminar."

"But why?" Mitch asked. "You said you loved it."

"Because I don't have any talent, Mitch!" Kelly

said. "Now, could you just move away, please? I have to go."

"Wait a second, Kelly. Let's talk about this. I—"

"Please!" Kelly was afraid she was about to burst into tears. She turned on the engine.

"Kelly—," Mitch said.

"I have to go, Mitch!" Kelly said. She raced the engine and Mitch moved away. Kelly stepped on the gas and took off.

▼ ▲ ▼

"I hope you don't mind having an early dinner," Jeff told Lisa. "I have a pile of studying to do when I get home."

"No problem," Lisa said. "This week has been so exhausting, I wouldn't mind getting to bed early."

Smiling, Lisa took a sip of tea. Jeff had been right. She just hadn't ordered the right things in a Thai restaurant before. Tonight, they'd had tiny, delicious egg rolls and an incredibly tasty soup flavored with mint. Now they were sharing a spicy shrimp-and-noodle dish.

Jeff seemed kind of distracted, but Lisa figured that he had had a pretty tough week, too. It was easy to concentrate on the food and not talk too much.

"It feels like all my friends are mad at me," Lisa admitted, spearing a shrimp. "Except you," she said with a smile.

Jeff twirled some noodles on his fork. "Is your friend Jessie one of the people who's mad at you?"

"You bet," Lisa said.

"Because of me?"

"Well . . . ," Lisa said. "No. Because of me, really. She doesn't know you like I do, Jeff. She doesn't trust you yet."

Jeff looked at her. "You trust me, Lisa?"

She nodded. "I do. I know I don't know you very well. But I can tell you're a good person. You want to protect your grandfather. Jessie doesn't understand that."

Jeff looked out the window at the ocean. "I worshiped my grandfather when I was a kid," he said. "You'd never know it now, but he was a big, strong guy when he was younger. He taught me how to ride. He used to take me camping in the mountains. My dad was pretty busy when I was a kid. But Granddad always had time for me."

"He sounds nice," Lisa said. *No matter what Jessie said.*

"He's not perfect," Jeff said. "I mean, he's done some things that I don't like. Maybe you heard about some of them. I guess he was pretty prejudiced. But he was born in nineteen seventeen. People didn't know any better back then. And his father was certainly no saint."

Jeff sighed and looked out the window. "You know what the funny thing is, Lisa? When it came to one-on-one, he was never prejudiced at all. For instance, our housekeeper, Susana, came from Mexico. She has a daughter, Natalie. She's my sister's age. She practically grew up with us. When it came time for Natalie to decide on a college, she was too intimidated to apply to any really good schools. And she had better grades than my sister. My grandfather sat with her in the kitchen night after night and helped her fill out her college applications. And when she got into Yale, he was the one who talked her into going. He gave her a loan so she wouldn't have to take a part-time job. He did all that," Jeff said earnestly.

Lisa nodded slowly. She wasn't sure what Jeff was trying to tell her.

"So when people say he's a bigot, I think of those nights when he sat up with Natalie, and I just can't condemn him. Do you know what I mean, Lisa?" Jeff's voice was tinged with desperation. "He can't be all bad, can he?"

"Nobody is all bad," Lisa said. "Listen, even though I'm African American, I've got a few bigots in my family tree, too. That doesn't mean I don't love them."

"You *do* see what I mean," Jeff said.

Jeff seemed so agitated. Lisa smiled at him gently. "Of course," she said. She plucked a piece of shrimp off her plate and put it on his. "Now eat this delicious food before it gets cold."

Lisa took another sip of tea and smiled into Jeff's honey-colored eyes. She knew she'd been right about him. She'd known it all along.

▼ ▲ ▼

Jessie pulled off her sweatshirt and tossed it onto the couch. So much for hanging out at the local gym. She'd been hoping to catch sight of Slater during his workout, but he'd never shown up. All Jessie'd gotten for her pains was pain. She'd pulled a muscle in her arm trying some new weight machine.

She chewed nervously on her lip. She hoped Slater didn't have a date. He had every right to have a date, of course. It was Friday night. There were no strings between them anymore. She only wished there were. As a matter of fact, she wished she had a nice stout *rope.* She'd tie that stubborn, muscle-bound caveman to a chair and talk to him nonstop until he realized he had to start loving her again.

The red light on the answering machine was blinking. Jessie hated the little leap in her heart that happened whenever she saw it. *Maybe this time it'll be him,* a little voice always whispered in her ear. But it never was.

Sighing, Jessie pushed PLAY.

"Jessie? This is Mrs. Claude Culpepper from the Palisades Historical Society? It just occurred to me, dear, that perhaps you didn't know where the meeting was scheduled tonight. Just in case Jefferson wasn't able to get ahold of you, you know. And don't forget to tell that lovely friend of yours, Miss Turtle."

Jessie frowned. A meeting tonight? She'd thought it was next week.

"Since it's a special meeting, we're not meeting at the normal meeting place. Ooh, I just keep saying 'meeting' over and over, don't I?" Mrs. Culpepper giggled. "Oh, where was I? The meeting. Anyway, since you're not home, I guess you're on your way to the meeting! All right, then. Hmmm. I hate these machines. . . . All right. I'll see you at the meeting, dear."

Jessie heard the machine click off. She sank down onto the couch as the facts clicked slowly into her brain.

There was a special meeting of the Palisades Historical Society.

It was being held in a new location.

She and Lisa had not been invited.

Jeff was supposed to have invited them and he hadn't.

"Double cross!" Jessie groaned.

Chapter 11

▼ ▲ ▼ ▲ ▼

Even with the covers over her head, Kelly heard the soft tapping at her bedroom door. She raised her head irritably.

"Who is it? Go away."

"It's me, honey," her mother said.

"Oh. Sorry, Mom. I'm really tired, okay? I don't want any dinner."

"Sweetheart, Zack is here to see you."

"Oh. Tell him I'm sleeping."

Suddenly, Zack's deeper voice boomed through the door. "Are you *talking* in your sleep?"

"Darn," Kelly said under her breath. "Zack, I'm really tired. I'll call you tomorrow, okay?"

"No," Zack said, opening the door.

He switched on the light. Kelly sat up, blinking. He grinned. "You look mmmarrvelous," he said teasingly.

Kelly glanced over at the mirror. Her hair was sticking up with static electricity, and she wasn't wearing any makeup. She was wearing her brother Kerry's old football jersey with a hole in the sleeve.

"Ready for our date, I see," Zack said.

Kelly bit her lip. She'd forgotten that she was supposed to go to the movies with Zack tonight.

"I'm sorry," she said. "I forgot all about it."

Zack sat down gingerly at the end of the bed. "I guess you're still mad at me, huh."

"I'm not mad at you, Zack," Kelly said. "I mean, I *was* mad. I'm sorry I yelled at you and the gang yesterday. Especially since you were right." To her horror, Kelly burst into tears.

Zack scooted over until he could put an arm around her. He squeezed her gently while she cried. When her sobs got quieter, he reached over for a handful of tissues and handed them to her. Kelly wiped her cheeks and blew her nose.

"Feel better?" he asked gently.

"A little," Kelly admitted.

"Because that red nose is really adding to your attractive outfit this evening," Zack said.

Kelly laughed. She blew her nose again. "Oh, Zack. You can always make me laugh. No matter how miserable I am."

"Can you tell me what happened?" Zack asked.

Kelly took a deep breath and spilled out the story of the audition. She told Zack everything, what the director had said and what Murray had said. She ended with her discussion with Mitch in the parking lot and what she'd told him. Then she blew her nose again.

"So you guys were right," she said. "I *do* stink up the joint."

Zack frowned. "Wait a second, Kelly. Maybe we were all too hasty. Screech swears that he thought you were okay. Maybe you got better since I saw you."

"But I did my very best at the audition, and I *still* stunk!" Kelly said.

"Maybe you were thrown off because of what happened at school," Zack suggested.

Kelly shook her head. "I felt completely calm and collected."

"Well, maybe the part was wrong for you," Zack tried. "Maybe you just couldn't relate to it."

"I played a teenage girl with a boyfriend who lies to get out of being caught doing something wrong and she swallows his story even though it's completely wild and crazy," Kelly said dryly.

"Oh," Zack said in a small voice. "I guess you might, uh, have some experience with that."

Kelly sighed. "Face it, Zack. I have. I'm not good at anything."

"I don't believe that," Zack said.

"Well, I do," Kelly sniffed.

Zack sat, his arms around Kelly. He struggled with his conscience. He knew the best advice for Kelly, but he wasn't crazy about giving it to her. Why should he send his girlfriend to a guy who was older, taller, and slightly cuter than he was?

But when he saw Kelly miserable, his heart felt like it was a contestant in a kick-boxing match. All he wanted to do was put the smile back on her face.

He squeezed her shoulder gently. "I know what you should do, Kelly. You should talk to Mitch."

"I did already," Kelly said miserably. "I quit the seminar. I told you."

"Talk to him again," Zack urged. "He's the only person who can make you feel better."

"*You* make me feel better," Kelly said with a wobbly smile.

He smiled back. "I'm glad. But Mitch is your teacher. Why don't you ask him for an honest evaluation? Maybe he *does* think you have talent."

Zack shifted around until he was facing her. "Kelly, you just started acting lessons last week.

How can you, or me, or Jessie, or any of us judge? Talk to Mitch. Or else you might wonder if you let go of a dream too easily."

"I don't know," Kelly said uncertainly. "I was pretty mean to him today."

"All the more reason to go," Zack said.

Suddenly, Kelly threw her arms around Zack. "You're right. Oh, Zack, I love you."

Zack hugged her back. Now he knew for sure he'd made the right decision.

▼ ▲ ▼

Jeff paid the check while Lisa took her last sip of tea. "Would you like to take a walk on the beach?" Lisa suggested. "The sun is starting to set."

Jeff looked uncomfortable. "Listen, Lisa. There's something I need to tell you."

"What is it?" Lisa asked. "I thought we straightened everything out. I understand why you feel you have to protect your family."

"You do?" Jeff said, his eyes searching hers. He reached across the table and captured her hand. "Because—"

Suddenly, the door to the restaurant burst open. Jessie stood in the doorway. She saw Lisa and Jeff and stalked over to their table. She gave their entwined hands a contemptuous look.

"Jessie, what are you doing here?" Lisa asked. She defiantly kept her hand in Jeff's, but slowly, his fingers slid out of her grasp.

"Maybe you should ask *him* that question," Jessie said, flicking her icy gaze at Jeff.

"What are you *talking* about? We've gone over this already," Lisa said.

"No, we haven't, Lisa," Jessie said. "Not this." She glanced at Jeff. "Are you proud of your scheme?"

"What scheme?" Lisa asked. What was Jessie talking about? And why wouldn't Jeff say anything?

"There's a historical society meeting tonight," Jessie informed Lisa. "A special one was called. And I have a feeling that Jeff's job is to keep us from it. Because they're probably discussing Wesley Racine Day!"

Lisa felt as though someone had punched her. She had trouble getting a breath. She looked steadily at Jeff. "Is that true, Jeff?"

"Yes," Jeff said. He didn't look at her.

Lisa stood up and threw her napkin on the table. "Let's go, Jessie. We have to get to that meeting."

"We can't," Jessie said. "I don't know where it is. It's not at the town hall. I called around, but none of the members are home. They all must be at the meeting."

"I can't believe this," Lisa said. "You were right, Jessie. I *am* stupid."

"Don't you dare blame yourself," Jessie said. "It's his fault." She turned to Jeff angrily. "I hope you realize how Lisa defended you. She *believed* in you and trusted you. You don't deserve someone as good as her!"

"I know that," Jeff said.

Jessie snorted contemptuously. She didn't believe his guilty act for one second.

"Let's go, Lisa," she said.

Jeff stood up. "Wait," he said.

"For what? More lies? You planned this all out, didn't you," Jessie said in disgust.

"No," Jeff said. "My grandfather did."

"You asked me out because your grandfather told you to?" Lisa asked. She felt tears sting her eyes, but she was determined not to cry.

"No, Lisa," Jeff said earnestly. "I asked you out because I wanted to go out with you. Then I put the papers back in the archives. But my grandfather already knew what you'd discovered. He was the one who'd found the Salazar letter in the first place. He'd stuck it in the old ledger until he could figure out what to do with it. I'd offered the archives to you without first telling him, so he hadn't had a chance to take it back."

"You mean your grandfather knew about the swindle?" Lisa asked.

"The project he's working on is a *revised* Racine history," Jeff said. "I realized that last night when I talked to him. He's going through the papers and taking out all the things that would embarrass the family."

"What about the meeting tonight?" Jessie asked suspiciously. "What's it all about?"

"And why couldn't we be there?" Lisa asked.

Jeff looked at Lisa. "When Grandfather found out I had a date with you, he called the meeting for the same night and told me not to tell you about it. He invited the city council members, too. He's going to get their support for Wesley Racine Day. Then they'll vote on it next week. By the time you went to the historical society meeting next week, it would be a done deal."

"And we wouldn't have had any proof for our accusations because Lisa had given you back the papers," Jessie said.

"You did what he told you to do," Lisa said woodenly.

"I'm not used to saying no to him," Jeff said. "He's not a man you say no to. Even my father can't. That's what I was trying to explain before, Lisa. I'm talking about *family.*" Jeff looked at her pleadingly.

Lisa looked away. "I'm talking about truth, Jeff. Integrity. Stuff like that."

"Stuff you wouldn't know about, Racine," Jessie said. "Lisa, let's get out of here. Jeff's grandfather has probably destroyed the papers. And he's probably talking the city council into Wesley Racine Day right now. It's too late to do anything about it."

"No, it isn't," Jeff said. "I can take you to the meeting."

"Where is it?" Lisa asked.

"It's at my house," he said.

"We don't need you to take us," Jessie countered. "We can get there ourselves."

"I'm afraid you do need me. You won't get past the gates otherwise." Jeff looked at them. "I can't speak out against my grandfather. But I can get you inside. Will you let me take you?"

Lisa and Jessie exchanged glances. "All right," Lisa said reluctantly. "You can take us. But after tonight, Jeff Racine, I never want to see you again!"

Chapter 12

▼ ▲ ▼ ▲ ▼

Nobody said a word as Jeff drove up the twisting mountain road. Lisa sat on the backseat, looking out the window. She felt like such a fool! Jessie had been right. When it came to boys, she didn't even have *half* a brain.

She could tell out of the corner of her eye that Jeff was sneaking looks at her in the rearview mirror. She supposed that it *was* decent of him to help them crash the meeting. She was sure he'd be in big trouble with his grandfather.

Jessie would probably say, *Big deal! He owes us. He's still a low-down, dirty swamp thing.*

Lisa sighed. The problem was that *she* didn't think Jeff was a low-down, dirty swamp thing. He was just a guy who was used to obeying his family, no matter what. Maybe that made him weak. But it didn't make him a horrible person. Maybe this experience would change him. Maybe taking this step would give him the guts to speak up once in a while.

Grow up, Lisa, Jessie would say. *You can take the thing out of the swamp, but you can't take the swamp out of the thing.*

"Here we are," Jeff said. He pressed a button on a transmitter, and the fancy iron gates slowly swung open. He turned down the curving road toward the house.

When they drove up, they saw that the paved area near the garage was packed with cars. Jeff eased his car in beside a Mercedes.

"What are you going to do?" Lisa asked him.

Jessie turned around and shot her a look from the front seat. *Why should you care?* the look said scornfully.

"I'll wait here for you," he said, not meeting her eyes. "The meeting is by the pool."

Lisa and Jessie got out of the car. Their footsteps crunched across the gravel as they headed toward the side of the house.

"He doesn't want to risk his grandfather finding out he brought us," Jessie said, swiping at a tree branch.

"At least he *did* bring us," Lisa said.

"I can't believe you're still making excuses for him," Jessie said.

Lisa pressed her lips together. She didn't want to argue with Jessie. There were more important things ahead.

They skirted the house and then walked down the dark lawn toward the pool. Flickering torches surrounded the area, and they saw white-jacketed waiters moving among the tables.

"Madison went all out," Jessie murmured. "Smart. Give them a swell party and a peek at the magnificent wealth of the mighty Racines."

Lisa gazed down at the sight. The tiny lights of Palisades twinkled below. The sky was a deep, dark blue, and the first stars were starting to appear. A bone white moon was beginning to rise. She'd imagined this scene before, but in her vision, she had been sitting poolside enjoying the romantic dusk with Jeff. She never thought she'd be there blowing his family apart.

"Ready?" Jessie asked grimly.

"Ready," Lisa said.

No one noticed them as they drifted through the trees and alongside the pool. They found seats at a table in the back.

They were just in time. Madison Racine got up from the first table, a small microphone in his hand. Tonight, he looked robust and healthy. A breeze stirred his white hair, and he raised an arm for quiet.

"Welcome, friends," he said. "And thank you. All of the Racines are touched and grateful that the members of the Palisades Historical Society have chosen to honor Wesley Racine. And, may I add, after having taken a very informal poll this evening, I have no doubt that the proposal will pass the city council."

The crowd erupted into polite applause. "Here, here," someone said.

"No way, no way," Jessie muttered.

She stood up. "Excuse me," she called in a clear, loud voice. "Mr. Racine? I have a question."

Madison Racine peered out through the crowd. He couldn't seem to see Jessie clearly. "Yes?" he asked politely.

"Actually, it's a question for your guests," Jessie said. She turned to the crowd. "Do we really want to honor a man who swindled his land from a local Mexican family that had been here for generations?"

Over the crowd's murmur, Lisa stood up next to Jessie. "And who then tried to pass a law that outlawed anyone of Mexican descent from the town?"

The murmur rose. People leaned across tables

to talk to their neighbors. Mrs. Claude Culpepper shook her head.

"This is a ridiculous charge!" Madison Racine thundered. "Wesley Racine bought this land fair and square. I have the original deed!"

"But the deed doesn't say how he *got* the land," Jessie countered.

"That's enough," Madison said. "Ladies and gentleman, the night air is chilly. Let's adjourn to the house for coffee and cake."

"If we allow this to happen, we'd be sending a message about our indifference to prejudice—" Jessie tried to say. But Madison Racine had the microphone, and he was urging the guests toward the house.

"Come, come," he was saying. "I'll explain everything inside."

"If he gets everyone inside, we'll never get to tell them the truth," Lisa muttered. "It will be too late."

"He's really good at damage control," Jessie said.

Some people started to move toward the house, but everyone else milled about, confused. Lisa waited until Madison stopped talking. Then she shouted, "We researched this. We have proof!"

Madison turned toward her. "What proof,

young lady?" he boomed. "You young people are always flying off the handle, looking to dirty the names of the great men who made this state what it is today, and I for one won't stand for it! Now, ladies and gentlemen, if you'd please—"

"Stop!" The voice came from behind them. Lisa's heart began to beat faster. She turned and saw Jeff standing on the edge of the lawn.

He walked forward a few steps. "There is proof," he said, his voice carrying in the sudden quiet. "And I've seen it."

He stood, his feet planted far apart, facing his grandfather. A breeze stirred his hair, and his eyes were blazing. He must have been nervous, but Lisa couldn't see it. He stood there, erect and calm. He reminded her of someone, and she realized with a shock who it was. His grandfather.

A couple who'd been sitting at Madison's table stood up slowly. Lisa recognized the familiar Racine features on the man. It must be Jeff's father, Abraham Lincoln Racine.

"Father?" he said, looking at Madison.

The pretty woman at his side looked at Jeff. "What is this?" she said. "What's going on, Jeff?"

"Granddad knows the charges are true," Jeff told his parents. "He's either hidden the papers or destroyed them. I'm sorry I have to do this, Mom and Dad. I love my family, but I don't have to support the bad things they did." He looked at his grandfather again, and this time, Jeff's voice was steely. "I *won't* support them."

Madison Racine held his grandson's gaze. There was some kind of battle going on between them, and the crowd waited, hushed, to see what would happen. Would Madison explode? Would Jeff crumble?

Very slowly, Madison Racine's shoulders began to slump. He dropped his gaze and looked down. He reached for the cane leaning against the table. He looked like an old man again.

"I think we should adjourn to the house," Jeff's father said to the crowd. "Please stay, everyone. Let's try to forget this unfortunate incident. *And* forget the notion of a Wesley Racine Day. I trust my son's judgment. The Racines have some reevaluating to do."

Jeff moved off to talk to his parents. The crowd began to slowly move toward the French doors of the house.

"Whew," Jessie said. "That was close."

"Too close for comfort," Lisa agreed. Her eyes were on Jeff as he shook hands with his father. His mother embraced him. But his grandfather turned away. Madison stalked off toward the house.

"We couldn't have done it without Jeff," Lisa said. "That took a lot of guts."

"I guess it did," Jessie admitted. "His grandfather definitely doesn't look like the forgiving kind."

The patio was quiet. Jeff's parents moved off toward the house. The waiters began clearing the tables.

"It looks like Jeff is waiting for you," Jessie said.

Lisa looked over. Jeff still stood by the first table. He was staring out over the twinkling lights of Palisades.

"You're going to forgive him, aren't you," Jessie said.

"Maybe," Lisa said. She looked at Jessie. "Will you think it's a no-brainer move if I do?"

Jessie sighed. "He tried to double-cross us. What would have happened if I hadn't shown up, Lisa?"

"I think Jeff would have told me the truth," Lisa answered. "Look, Jessie, you were right. I didn't really have a reason to trust Jeff in the beginning. But something happened between us tonight at dinner. I really got to know him. And I guess I still have faith in him. I think he deserves another chance. Maybe you think that's stupid. But I don't."

Jessie looked away, down the valley to the lights of Palisades. *Faith.* She'd heard that word before. *You just don't have faith in me, Jess,* Slater had said to her when he'd broken up with her. *And that's the end of the line for me.*

It was funny. That last time they'd been together, Slater had tried to talk to her, and she'd only been able to argue with him. Although she'd just kept telling him she loved him and wouldn't he give her another chance, she hadn't really *listened* to him.

Faith. It was like a secret she hadn't been let in on, Jessie thought, heartsick. Lisa knew the secret. Slater knew the secret. But Jessie had been too stubborn, too defensive to see it.

Somehow, Lisa had taught her what Slater had been trying to tell her all along. You had to have a little faith in people. It was as simple, and as hard, as that.

She turned to her friend. "I don't think you're an idiot at all, Lisa," she said softly. "I think you're the smartest person around. Now go on. Talk to Jeff. He's waiting."

▼ ▲ ▼

On Saturday morning, Kelly drove north. She knew Mitch's address, and she drove to the beach town where he lived. She parked the car and knocked on his door, her heart thumping nervously.

A tall, redheaded guy answered the door with a long yawn. "Oops, sorry," he said. "Just woke up."

"Hi, Presley," Kelly said. "Do you remember me? I'm Kelly. I came to your party in New York."

Presley brightened. "Hey, I never forget a pretty face. And Mitch told me you were in his seminar. Come on in. Keep your eyes closed, though; the place is a mess. I'll just lead you to the living room."

Kelly laughed. "Is Mitch here?"

"No, he went to the beach. You can wait, if you want," Presley said quickly, when he saw Kelly's crestfallen face. "Only he might not be home for hours."

"Oh," Kelly said. "Maybe I should just head back. Could you tell him I was here, though?"

Presley brightened. "Hold on. Just go on down to the beach. It's only three blocks away. And you can't miss him. I'll tell you his favorite spot. Okay?"

"Okay," Kelly said, smiling at Presley's eagerness to please her. He was a really sweet guy.

Presley's directions were perfect. Kelly only had to walk a short distance on the soft sand before she saw Mitch. He was sitting in a beach chair wearing a red baseball cap, reading a script.

She walked up to him. "Hi," she said, feeling suddenly shy.

He looked up. "Kelly! Hi. What are you doing here? What a coincidence."

"Not really," Kelly said. "Presley told me where to find you. I really need to talk to you."

He nodded. "Have a seat in my office," he said, gesturing to his towel on the sand.

Kelly sat down. "I want to apologize about yesterday. I was really rude."

"Nah," Mitch said. "I only lost one toe when you took off."

Kelly grinned. "I'm really sorry about that."

"Well, we must be on the same wavelength," Mitch said. "Because I'm really sorry, too."

He put the script down in the sand and leaned toward her. "I handled things wrong. I tried to act like a teacher *and* a friend, and I guess I got mixed up. You got hurt. I feel really badly about that."

Kelly shook her head. "I was being a baby. I kept *saying* I wanted constructive criticism, but I really wanted everyone to tell me I was terrific. I was a complete amateur."

Mitch grinned. "You think professionals are any better?"

Kelly sighed and rested her chin on her knees. "I was mad at you because you didn't tell me I was bad. But I didn't give you a chance."

"Kelly, let me ask you something. Who told you that acting is easy?"

"I know it's not easy," she said ruefully. "I learned that this past week."

"No, you didn't," Mitch said. "If you *really* learned that it's not easy, you wouldn't be so down on yourself for not being good right at the start. You'd see that acting is a craft that can be learned. You wouldn't expect to paint like Picasso after one art class, would you?"

"I never thought about it like that," Kelly said slowly. "But, Mitch, acting isn't just about learning. It's about talent. And if you don't have any, no matter how much you learn, you'll still stink."

Mitch nodded. "True. But sometimes you can't see talent right off the bat. That's why I don't discourage *anybody.* That director yesterday might have told you the truth about your performance, but he had no right to tell you to quit. I can't tell you how many stars were told they'd never make it. There aren't many naturals in this business."

"But what if you keep trying and trying, and you never get better?" Kelly asked. "You'll just keep making a fool of yourself."

He leaned over and touched her nose. "That's your problem, kiddo."

"What?"

"You're afraid to make a fool of yourself. And that's what acting is all about. That risk. That's why you did so badly in the trust exercises. You didn't trust your fellow actors, and you didn't trust yourself. You were afraid. So you played it safe."

"But I could have fallen," Kelly protested.

Mitch shrugged. "That's the risk."

Kelly traced a pattern on the sand while she thought about Mitch's words. "But *do* I have any talent, Mitch?" she asked finally. "I have to *know*."

He grinned. "I'm not going to tell you that, Kelly." She opened her mouth, and he held up a hand. "Because number one, I honestly don't know. And number two, if you really want to be an actress, *you* have to believe it. No matter how much discouragement and bad breaks get thrown your way. Every actor has given a bad performance, Kelly. The trick is to learn from it and keep going. It's a tough profession, right from the start."

Kelly sighed. "Okay. I get it. I have to believe in myself." She grinned. "And I thought acting like a piece of sizzling bacon was hard."

Mitch grinned back. "So what do you say? Will you stay in the seminar? I'd hate to lose you."

She gazed at the water. Slowly, she nodded. "I'll stay. I'll keep trying. I guess I'm not ready to give up my dream yet."

"And you'll make a fool of yourself if you have to?" Mitch pressed.

"And I'll make a fool of myself if I have to," Kelly repeated.

Mitch sprang to his feet. He reached down and

offered her his hand. "Then come on. Let's start here."

"Here?" Kelly asked confusedly. "At the beach?"

He grinned. "It's the perfect place. You'll see."

Chapter 13

▼ ▲ ▼ ▲ ▼

One week later, Kelly peeked out from behind the curtains of the stage at Bayside High. She gulped as her eyes roamed over the seats filled with familiar faces. She could glimpse her parents and her four brothers and one sister sitting third row center. Zack, Jessie, Slater, and Lisa were sitting together right in front of them.

"Gosh," she murmured. "The place is packed."

"Just remember one thing," Riley McGee advised from behind her. "They can't eat you."

Kelly grinned, but she didn't feel any better. Riley McGee was the best actor in the Bayside Players. What did he have to worry about? He wasn't about to make a complete and utter fool of himself in the talent contest. He'd probably never given a bad performance in his life.

Mitch's voice rose in her head. *Every actor has given a bad performance, Kelly. The trick is to learn from it and keep going.*

Screech popped his head in from the wings. "Hey, guys. Ms. McCracken wants us all backstage. It's three minutes to curtain."

"Break a leg," Riley said to Kelly.

"If only I could," she moaned.

"And don't forget your neck, too!" Screech added.

▼ ▲ ▼

Kelly clenched her fists by her side. She didn't see the Bayside High stage. She didn't see the faces of her loving parents, or her brothers and sister, or her classmates. She saw the tense, angry face of a father who couldn't love his daughter.

"I'm gonna make it because nobody thinks I can," she said. At one time, she'd almost shouted the words. This time, her voice was pitched low. But its intensity carried it to the very last row of the auditorium.

"Maybe that's not a good reason. But it works for me. So I'll be moving out, Pop. If you ever happen to notice I'm gone, wish me well."

Kelly held the moment for just a beat, the way

Mitch had coached her. Then she stepped back and bowed.

The audience burst into applause. She saw her family clapping. And then she saw Zack, Jessie, Slater, and Lisa. They were clapping loudly, with stunned looks on their faces. She grinned. Now she knew she'd done okay. Her friends couldn't believe she'd given a decent performance.

Kelly knew in her heart that she hadn't been great. She'd been nervous at the beginning. But at least she'd ended well. And she hadn't humiliated herself in front of everyone at Bayside.

Kelly practically floated off the stage, her head high. She'd never felt so ecstatic in her life. She'd done it!

She watched the rest of the show from the wings. Screech came out and performed "Byte-size Fugue" on the school synthesizer. Kelly restrained herself from putting her hands over her ears. The song didn't have rhythm and it didn't have melody, but it did have enthusiasm.

After Screech finished, Kelly led the applause. It didn't matter if Screech's act was terrible or not, she knew now. It took guts just to get up there.

As Mitch would say, *You get points for just doing it.*

Finally, Ms. McCracken came onstage to announce the winners. Riley McGee and Melissa

Alden came in first for their sketch. Toby Welliver came in second for his hip-hop dance. And Greg Tolan came in third for singing and playing the guitar.

The rest of the contestants were called onstage and given a last round of applause. They laughed and bowed as the auditorium was rocked with cheers. And even though Kelly hadn't won, she felt great.

Screech and Kelly hurried out into the auditorium to meet the gang. They were waiting by the stage door and rushed up to Screech and Kelly to congratulate them both. Zack hugged Kelly.

"You were incredible," he said.

Kelly laughed. "I was okay," she said. "I was nervous in the beginning."

"You could tell, sort of," Jessie said. "But then, at the end, I forgot you were Kelly for a minute. You really were good."

"I can't believe how much you've improved," Lisa said.

"It was Mitch," Kelly said. "He really worked with me. All those trust exercises at the beach paid off."

Zack frowned. "Trust exercises?"

Jessie shot a glance at Slater. "Sounds like I could use a few of those." He looked at her, surprised.

"They're acting exercises," Kelly explained. "I couldn't loosen up to really do them. Then Mitch had this great idea. We did them in the water. I'd fall over backward and had to trust that he'd catch me. Or we'd do a body lift where he'd lift me over his head. We even brought the whole class down there. Being in the water made me feel safer, because I knew I wouldn't get hurt if someone dropped me. I got looser and looser, and pretty soon, I could do it on land. Somehow that really helped my performance."

"Sounds weird," Zack said. "But whatever works." He didn't think he was crazy about Kelly throwing herself into some other guy's arms at the beach. *Some other, taller, older, slightly cuter guy, that is.*

"Mitch is the best teacher," Kelly said, her eyes glowing. "I never could have done it without him."

"Mmmm," Zack said. Did Kelly have to look *quite* so grateful?

"Actually, I couldn't have done it without you, too," Kelly said to Zack.

"Thanks for remembering me," he growled.

She laughed happily. "If you hadn't told me to talk to Mitch, I would have just said forget it. And I would have really regretted it."

Suddenly, Mitch's head appeared above the crowd. Why did the guy have to be so *tall*?

"Mitch!" Kelly squealed.

He came up and hugged her. "You were great."

She smiled up at him. "Weak beginning, but an okay finish."

He laughed. "Tough critic," he said fondly. "Tomorrow we can dissect it, kiddo. Tonight—just enjoy it."

Zack's eyes narrowed. He didn't like that flush on Kelly's cheek. That sparkle in her eye. And he didn't like how handsome Mitch was, either. Sure, he was glad Kelly was so happy. But he wasn't sure about this acting thing. The trouble with the acting profession was that it was full of *actors.* Tall, well-built actors who were slightly cuter than he was.

Mitch said good-bye and moved off. With a happy sigh, Kelly watched him go.

Jessie moved to Zack's side. "Looks like you could use some trust exercises, too, Zack," she murmured in his ear. "Do you want me to lift you over my head?"

Zack grinned. "I'll let you know," he said.

"Well, to quote Willy Shakespeare, 'All's well that ends well,'" Jessie said philosophically, turning to the gang. "I think we all learned a valuable lesson."

"Never tell the truth?" Slater said, and everyone laughed.

"That the truth is a powerful force," Jessie said. "We should be careful how we use it."

"But we should try to tell it," Kelly said. "No matter how hard it is to hear."

"You said it," Lisa agreed. "Now that I'm dating Jeff, I'm always going to be honest with him."

"Speaking of the truth," Screech said, "what did you all think of my 'Byte-size Fugue'?"

The gang hesitated.

"Fantastic," Zack said.

"Incredible," Slater added.

"Fabulous," Lisa said with a nod.

"Just wonderful," Jessie said.

"Really, really amazing," Kelly finished.

Screech slung his arms around their shoulders. "Thanks, gang. I knew I could always count on my friends to tell me the truth!"